ALSO BY LIAN HEARN

TALES OF THE OTORI

Across the Nightingale Floor

Grass for His Pillow

Brilliance of the Moon

The Harsh Cry of the Heron

Heaven's Net Is Wide

Blossoms and Shadows

The Storyteller and His Three Daughters

THE TALE OF SHIKANOKO

Emperor of the Eight Islands

AUTUMN PRINCESS,
DRAGON CHILD

THE TALE OF SHIKANOKO · BOOK 2

AUTUMN PRINCESS, DRAGON CHILD

LIAN HEARN

FARRAR, STRAUS AND GIROUX   NEW YORK

Farrar, Straus and Giroux
18 West 18th Street, New York 10011

Copyright © 2016 by Lian Hearn Associates Pty Ltd.
All rights reserved
Printed in the United States of America
Originally published in 2016 by Hachette Australia
Published in the United States by Farrar, Straus and Giroux
First American edition, 2016

Map by K1229 Design

Library of Congress Cataloging-in-Publication Data
Names: Hearn, Lian, author.
Title: Autumn Princess, Dragon Child / Lian Hearn.
Description: First American edition. | New York : Farrar, Straus and
    Giroux, 2016. | Series: The tale of Shikanoko series ; 2
Identifiers: LCCN 2015042557 | ISBN 9780374536329 (softcover)
    | ISBN 9780374715021 (ebook)
Subjects: LCSH: Japan—History—1185–1600—Fiction.
    | BISAC: FICTION / Literary. | FICTION / Fantasy / General.
    | GSAFD: Fantasy fiction. | Adventure fiction. | Historical fiction.
Classification: LCC PR9619.3.H3725 A96 2016 | DDC 823/.914—dc23
LC record available at http://lccn.loc.gov/2015042557

Designed by Jonathan D. Lippincott

Our books may be purchased in bulk for promotional, educational, or
business use. Please contact your local bookseller or the Macmillan
Corporate and Premium Sales Department at 1-800-221-7945, extension
5442, or by e-mail at MacmillanSpecialMarkets@macmillan.com.

www.fsgbooks.com • www.fsgoriginals.com
www.twitter.com/fsgbooks • www.facebook.com/fsgbooks

10   9   8   7   6   5   4   3   2   1

I will gather up
The transparent beads scattered
By the waterfall
And borrow them when sadness
Has consumed my store of tears.

—from *Kokin Wakashū: The First
Imperial Anthology of Japanese
Poetry*, translated by Helen Craig
McCullough

THE TALE OF SHIKANOKO
LIST OF CHARACTERS

MAIN CHARACTERS

Kumayama no Kazumaru, later known as Shikanoko or
   Shika

Nishimi no Akihime, the Autumn Princess, **Aki**

Kuromori no **Kiyoyori**, the Kuromori lord

Lady **Tama**, his wife, the Matsutani lady

Masachika, Kiyoyori's younger brother

Hina, sometimes known as Yayoi, his daughter

Tsumaru, his son

Bara or Ibara, Hina's servant

Yoshimori, also Yoshimaru, the Hidden Emperor, **Yoshi**

Takeyoshi, also Takemaru, son of Shikanoko and
   Akihime, **Take**

Lady **Tora**

Shisoku, the mountain sorcerer

Sesshin, an old wise man

The **Prince Abbot**

Akuzenji, King of the Mountain, a bandit

Hisoku, Lady Tama's retainer

THE MIBOSHI CLAN

Lord **Aritomo**, head of the clan, also known as the
    Minatogura lord

Yukikuni no **Takaakira**

The **Yukikuni lady**, his wife

Takauji, their son

Arinori, lord of the Aomizu area, a sea captain

Yamada Keisaku, Masachika's adoptive father

Gensaku, one of Takaakira's retinue

Yasuie, one of Masachika's men

Yasunobu, his brother

THE KAKIZUKI CLAN

Lord **Keita**, head of the clan

Hosokawa no **Masafusa**, a kinsman of Kiyoyori

Tsuneto, one of Kiyoyori's warriors

Sadaike, one of Kiyoyori's warriors

Tachiyama no **Enryo**, one of Kiyoyori's warriors

Hatsu, his wife

Kongyo, Kiyoyori's senior retainer

Haru, his wife

Chikamáru, later Motochika, **Chika**, his son

Kaze, his daughter

Hironaga, a retainer at Kuromori
Tsunesada, a retainer at Kuromori
Taro, a servant in Kiyoyori's household in Miyako

THE IMPERIAL COURT
The **Emperor**
Prince Momozono, the Crown Prince
Lady Shinmei'in, his wife, Yoshimori's mother
Daigen, his younger brother, later Emperor
Lady Natsue, Daigen's mother, sister to the Prince Abbot
Yoriie, an attendant
Nishimi no **Hidetake**, Aki's father, foster father
    to Yoshimori
Kai, his adopted daughter

AT THE TEMPLE OF RYUSONJI
Gessho, a warrior monk
Eisei, a young monk, later one of the **Burnt Twins**

AT KUMAYAMA
Shigetomo, Shikanoko's father
Sademasa, his brother, Shikanoko's uncle, now lord
    of the estate
Nobuto, one of his warriors
Tsunemasa, one of his warriors
Naganori, one of his warriors

Nagatomo, Naganori's son, Shika's childhood friend, later one of the **Burnt Twins**

Lady Sadako and **Lady Masako**, Hina's teachers
Saburo, a groom

Lady Fuji, the mistress of the pleasure boats
Asagao, a musician and entertainer
Yuri, **Sen**, **Sada**, and **Teru**, young girls at the convent
Sarumaru, **Saru**, an acrobat and monkey trainer
Kinmaru and **Monmaru**, acrobats and monkey trainers

Kiku, later Master Kikuta, Lady Tora's oldest son
Mu, her second son
Kuro, her third son
Ima, her fourth son
Ku, her fifth son
Tsunetomo, a warrior, Kiku's retainer
Shida, Mu's wife, a fox woman
Kinpoge, their daughter

Unagi, a merchant in Kitakami

SUPERNATURAL BEINGS
Tadashii, a tengu
Hidari and **Migi**, guardian spirits of Matsutani
The dragon child
Ban, a flying horse
Gen, a fake wolf
Kon and **Zen**, werehawks

HORSES
Nyorin, Akuzenji's white stallion, later Shikanoko's
Risu, a bad-tempered brown mare
Tan, their foal

WEAPONS
Jato, Snake Sword
Jinan, Second Son
Ameyumi, Rain Bow
Kodama, Echo

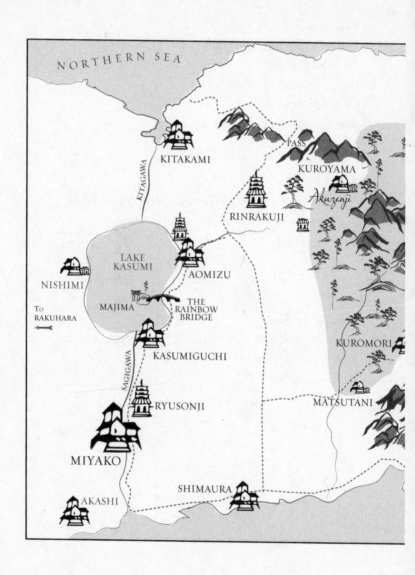

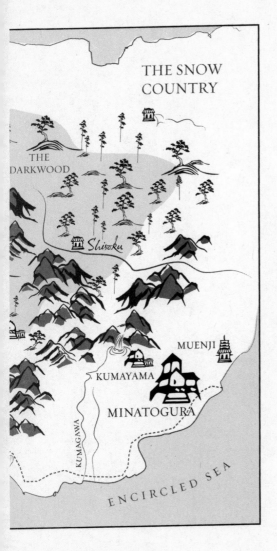

THE SNOW
COUNTRY

THE
DARKWOOD

Shisoku

MUENJI

KUMAYAMA

MINATOGURA

KUMAGAWA

ENCIRCLED SEA

----- ROADS

——— RIVERS
AND STREAMS

CONVENT
OR TEMPLE

HUT

SHRINE

ESTATE

TOWN

AUTUMN PRINCESS, DRAGON CHILD

SHIKANOKO

Shikanoko, unable to sleep, racked by pain and fever, walked day and night through the Darkwood. His flesh alternately froze and burned; it did not seem to belong to him. He floated outside his body, watching it sweat and shiver, wondering why it still clung to life. Often he hallucinated. The dead seemed to walk alongside him, haranguing and accusing him. Once he heard the horses' shrill neighing, and did not know whether to run to them or hide from them. His weapons, and the bag holding the broken mask and Kiyoyori's sword, grew heavier. One day he simply let his own sword and the bow and quiver fall to the ground. He could not imagine ever using them again. The following day he was tortured by the smell of death. *I am rotting away*, he thought. *It is all over.* He leaned against the smooth trunk of a young beech tree, and then half-fell, half-slid down it until he was sitting in the dried leaves at its foot. The forest, in high summer, reverberated around him with bird calls and insect cries. Once he had loved that sound, had known every bird. Now it was an unpleasant clamor that made his head ache.

He had buried his head in his arms, but now a sudden strange sound, a kind of rough bark, made him look up. A crafted animal, a sort of wolf, stood before him. He saw the flash of its lapis blue eyes and the dull gleam of its cinnabar lips. The clarity of the hallucination and his fever filled him with despair.

Then the false wolf spoke in a thick, halting voice. "Welcome home," it said, and Shika knew where he was and where the stench of rot and decay came from. It was over a year since he had ridden away with Akuzenji, the King of the Mountain, but now he had come back, to the mountain sorcerer, Shisoku.

It watched him struggle to his feet and then turned and padded stiffly away. He followed it, across the stream, past the carvings, the drying skins, the piles of bones, the live and dead animals, to the hut beneath the paulownia tree.

It stopped in front of the door. "Master!" it called. The vowels in its speech were clear, but it had trouble with some consonants: *Ma-er!*

Shisoku came out of the hut, shading his eyes with one hand.

"Shikanoko? Why have you come back? What have you done?"

Shika dropped the bag as Shisoku approached him. It

lay on the ground like a dead bird, the hilt of the sword protruding from it.

"What is this? Whose sword was this? Nothing should be put in the same bag as the mask! Where is the mask?"

"It is broken," Shika heard himself say.

"Aaargh!" Shisoku screamed like the mother of a dead child. "It cannot be broken. No human power can hurt it. How did it happen?"

He drew the two pieces out and wept over them.

Shika tried to explain. "It was the horses, they attacked me; not their fault, my fault."

Shisoku's face was distorted by rage and grief. Without saying another word he rushed back into the hut. Shika sank to the ground. His teeth clashed against each other as the fever sent violent shudders through him.

"Are you sick?" the false wolf said. "Master, he's sick."

"Let him die," Shisoku called from inside. "He destroyed my gift, my creation. All the power of the forest could have been his, and he threw it away."

The false wolf called again. "Master, help him!" and it began to lick Shika's face with a tongue that felt human.

The sorcerer appeared again. "How extraordinary," Shika heard him say. "The creature feels sorry for him. Maybe I should, too. Yes, I suppose I must." He knelt next to Shika and felt his forehead, then, none too gently, examined the broken arm.

While Shika wept tears of pain, Shisoku disappeared and then, after what seemed like an eternity, was again kneeling beside him, making him drink some potion. It dulled his senses enough for Shisoku to be able to align the ends of the broken bone.

He longed for sleep, for oblivion, but every time he closed his eyes he believed he was dead and in Hell, burning in fire, pierced by swords, knives, arrows, and thorns, tormented by visions of demons and unquenchable thirst. He saw, over and over again, the horses' huge teeth as they tore into him, and his body arched and twisted as he felt again the hammerlike blows of their hooves.

Liquid poured from his body, both sweat and tears, the waters of remorse.

At one stage he dreamed Lady Tora came to him. "Are you alive or dead?" he tried to ask her, but she laid her cool fingers against his burning lips and silenced not only speech but thought, too.

Then finally he slept, maybe for days. All that time the false wolf did not leave his side.

When he woke, he was inside the hut; he heard Shisoku say, "It has become attached to him. It's the first time something like that has happened. I did not expect it. Even I have never inspired affection in my creations."

"You are a greater sorcerer than you think," a woman replied. Shika turned his head slightly and saw it was indeed Lady Tora. She went on, "Perhaps it is because you bestowed the power of speech on it. How did you achieve that?"

Shisoku laughed. "I gave it the tongue I cut from a human head, and I built speaking cords from gossamer and sinews."

"And the head? Whose was that?"

"There have been plenty of dead between Miyako and Minatogura in the last year. This was a Kakizuki warrior who fled into the forest and died of his wounds. I came upon him while he was still fresh enough to use. That's his skull on the wall."

Shika could see the new white skull grinning vacantly. Next to him the false wolf whined.

"Shikanoko is awake," Lady Tora said.

They both looked in his direction. Their shapes were outlined against the flames of the fire and the candles around the altar. He saw the huge swell of Tora's belly and remembered what she had told him, that she would give Kiyoyori more sons. Whoever's child it was, it was very close to birth.

"Shisoku was extremely angry with you," Lady Tora said, "but he has forgiven you now."

"I have?" the hermit queried.

"Either you have or you soon will. But Shikanoko should tell us what happened. See if you can get up," she said to him.

He struggled to his feet and, leaning on Shisoku and Lady Tora, went outside. They led him to the paulownia tree and, sitting between them in its shade, he related everything, from the blinding of Sesshin to their flight into the Darkwood, their capture by his uncle Sademasa, who handed them over to the monk Gessho, the knowledge Sesshin had passed over to him, the winter spent at Ryusonji with the Prince Abbot.

7

"There was an uprising," he said. "Well, it was started by the Prince Abbot, who dispatched his men to arrest the Crown Prince, but afterward it was said that Momozono rebelled against his father. He died, but his son escaped. I was sent to find him and bring his head back to the capital. I caught up with him, and Akihime, the Autumn Princess, on the way to Rinrakuji."

"Ah," Lady Tora said. "Now I begin to understand."

"I killed two men who were about to violate her and the young Emperor, for he truly is the Emperor, you know. Everything recognizes him. I had two werehawks with me and they knew him at once. I called them Kon and Zen. Zen tried to fly back to Ryusonji and Kon killed him. We rode on toward Rinrakuji, but we were stopped at a crossroads by a spirit. It was Lord Kiyoyori."

"So he is dead?" Tora said, in a small voice.

"I called him back," Shika said, remembering the immense power that he had drawn on, a power that had led him into pride and arrogance and betrayed him. "His spirit entered the unborn foal within the body of my mare, Risu."

"He drove the horses to attack you?" Lady Tora said.

"Yes, and that is how the mask was broken."

He fell silent, and then said, "The sword is Kiyoyori's. It is beyond repair, too."

"Nothing is beyond repair for Shisoku," Tora said. "Even if the results are sometimes unexpected, like this false wolf that has attached itself to you."

It must recognize my falseness, Shikanoko thought. *We are two of a kind.* But his confession was not finished yet.

"We went to Akuzenji's old hut. I was planning to bring them here to hide them."

"The last place you would expect to find the Emperor of the Eight Islands," Shisoku muttered.

Shika went on steadily, "But being in the hut, alone with the Autumn Princess, who I thought was the one meant for me, I put on the mask and found myself under the Prince Abbot's sway. I blame only myself. I thought I was all powerful . . ."

"Aha!" Shisoku said. "He could teach you many things, but he could not teach you brokenness."

Shika wished he would stop interrupting. Every time he had to start again it was harder.

"The Prince Abbot told me to do what I liked with her. I did. But she was to become a shrine maiden. She fled during the night. In the morning he told me to kill Yoshimori, and I was on the point of doing it, when the werehawk and the horses attacked me. When I came to, I was alone and the mask was broken."

"The gods must have been enraged against you both," Tora said.

After a few moments Shika said, "The werehawk, Kon, was turning gold. I remember seeing the sun on its plumage."

"It must be transforming into a houou," Shisoku said. "It is the sacred bird that appears in the land when the ruler is just and blessed by Heaven."

"That must be Yoshimori. I have to find him and restore him to the throne."

"This is a concern of warriors and noblemen," Shisoku said. "Leave them to it and become a mountain sorcerer like me."

"I was a warrior first, long before I became a sorcerer," Shika replied. "Restore the mask for me, and the sword, and, when they are ready, I will begin my search for Yoshimori."

"Nothing will change until your power matches the Prince Abbot's," Lady Tora said. "You are going to have to confront him and overcome him physically and spiritually. At the moment you can do neither. You have no men, no followers, not even a horse. In your first challenge to him, you failed. He forced you to make a terrible mistake, from which you may never recover. The horses and the were-hawk, which should have been your allies, turned against you. You have a lot to undo and even more to learn."

"How long will it take you to repair the mask and the sword?" Shika asked Shisoku.

"When you are ready they will be ready," the old man replied grudgingly.

"Will it be days or weeks?"

"More likely years," said the sorcerer.

"I can't wait that long," Shika cried, his impatience signaling he was recovering.

Lady Tora said, "There will be plenty to occupy you. As well as all you have to learn, you have to bring up my sons."

"That will teach you something," Shisoku murmured.

❋

"The children cannot come into the world here," Lady Tora said, "in the midst of Shisoku's wayward magic, all these bones, skins, and transmogrification."

"Certainly not," Shisoku agreed. "Childbirth, especially involving one of the Old People, is completely disruptive and would unleash all kinds of uncontrollable forces, though possibly I could use some of those to repair the mask, so don't go too far away."

"Shikanoko must help me build a dwelling," she said.

The Old People . . . where had he heard that before? Then Sesshin's words crystalized in his mind. Just after he had transferred the nugget of power into Shika's mouth he had said, *From five fathers five children will be born. Find them and destroy them. They will be demons. She is one of the Old People.*

The words haunted him as, under her instructions, he built a small hut on the north side of the clearing, facing south. He cut the wood, from sweet-smelling maples and strong holm oaks, with Shisoku's sharp-edged axe and saw.

Shika had never built anything before, and like most of Shisoku's endeavors, the results were not quite what was expected, but he liked the process of hewing the wood and shaping it into a human dwelling. It was like making bows and arrows, a kind of magic in itself, turning what the forest gave into something that had not existed before. When it was finished, and thatched with susuki reeds, it looked very pleasing.

Shisoku treated the tools as if they were children or servants. He never took them down from their place on the wall without asking their permission or put them back without thanking them. Shika saw how everything in his world was connected, how he knew intimately all the unseen strands and interstices, and how his power came from that knowledge, his ability to unravel and reconnect.

At the time when the silkworms began to spin their cocoons, Lady Tora also began to spin. Shika did not see where the threads came from, perhaps the gossamer that the morning mist turned into bright jewels, mixed with the soft underbelly fur of wolf and fox, or from the long tendrils of wisteria and bryony, seeds of milkweed and dandelion, delicate and powerful strands of root and sinew of bark, everything pliable and tensile that could be turned into yarn.

From this she wove five cocoons, soft on the inside and hard on the outside, and hung them from the rafters of the hut. One morning, it was clear that each held some kind of egg.

Shika did not witness their birth nor did he hear any of the cries of pain that usually accompany childbirth. Lady Tora seemed exhausted. She did not want him near her, but lay all day without moving. From the door of the hut he could smell a distinctive odor of blood and egg yolk. At dusk, she asked Shika to bring water and rags and wait outside while she washed herself.

Afterward, she gave him the bowl, saying, "Give this to Shisoku. It is full of power."

Her voice was faint, her face pale, and she seemed to have been drained of something essential. Over the next few days, while the creatures in the cocoons grew, she faded.

"My work on earth is achieved," she told Shika when he tried to urge her to eat.

"Does she mean to die?" he asked the sorcerer.

Shisoku pursed his lips and then said reluctantly, "It is the way of the Old People."

"Who are the Old People?"

"Sometimes they are called the Spider Tribe. They are the ones who were here before."

"Before when?" Shika said.

"Before people like you came from Silla, with your swords and your horses, your princes and your emperors."

"I have never heard of them!" A suspicion came to him. "Are you one of them?"

"My grandmother was. She died when my father was born, from a cocoon like this. His father raised him in the forest, as we will have to raise these children. They will not be like ordinary children."

"Will they be demons?" Shika asked with a sort of dread.

Shisoku smiled. "Not demons, just different."

Shika had to ask. "And me? Am I one?"

"Because you came here at the right time? Because you were able to become the deer's child? I wondered sometimes, and so did Tora. But we did not know of you, and there are so few left, we know every one. Maybe there is some blood mixed in you. Maybe you were just lucky."

"Or unlucky," Shika said quietly.

"That, too," Shisoku agreed. "Did you ever cross paths with a tengu?"

Shikanoko was silent for a moment.

"Did you?"

"When I was a child, I vaguely remember something, but perhaps it was a dream. Why?"

"When you first came I thought I discerned some tengu influence in your life."

"In my dream, if that's what it was, my father played a game of Go with a tengu. He lost the game, his life, and Ameyumi, his bow. He left me hidden in the grass, but the tengu flew overhead and they saw me. I remember their beaks and their wings."

"Well, that's interesting," the sorcerer said. "That could explain a lot."

A few days later Lady Tora called them into the hut. The creatures had grown into human-looking infants, now too big for the cocoons, which were beginning to tear as the children struggled and pushed with their hands and feet.

"Shouldn't we help them get out?" Shika said.

"No, they must do it alone, so we know who is the first and strongest."

It seemed as though two would emerge at once, and even before the final rip of the silky fabric, they appeared to be racing against each other. They grew under Shika's eyes, and by the time the first child stood before them he was the size of a two-year-old, wobbling on uncertain legs like the young animals of the forest.

"You shall be called Kiku," Lady Tora said. "It means Listen. You will hear everything. Because you were the first to emerge you will be the strongest and the cleverest."

Almost immediately the second child was on his feet, looking around with inquisitive, unafraid eyes.

"Your name is Mu," his mother said. "Both Nothingness and Warrior. You will exist between the two. No one will see you. It is your fate always to strive to be first, but you will never overtake Kiku."

There was something enchanting about them. They were appealing, like fawns or baby monkeys.

"Come," Shika said, and took a boy in each arm. Mu's pressure on his broken arm caused only the slightest ache. It was almost completely healed.

The third child crawled from the cocoon and Lady Tora gave him the name Kuro, Darkness, and told him he would walk alone.

"He will be like me," Shisoku said, as he held him on his knee.

There was a short lull as the two remaining children struggled, with more difficulty, to emerge. The others watched, with no apparent emotion beyond curiosity. Shika felt the warmth of Kiku's and Mu's bodies as they rested with complete trust against him. They were beautiful beings, with thick black hair and slender limbs. He thought of the five fathers whose seed had combined to make them: Akuzenji, Kiyoyori, Sesshin, Shisoku, and himself. It was quite impossible for him to consider killing them.

One of the remaining two came free and crawled out, limp and exhausted. "Your name is Ima, Now," Lady

Tora said. "You will be a servant to your brothers, you will never know envy or disappointment." She embraced him for a moment before giving him to Shisoku.

"And it is your fate to be last," she said to the final child. He was noticeably smaller than the others and did not stand and walk immediately, but crawled on all fours, like a blind puppy. "Your name will be Ku. You will love all animals and they will love and trust you. You will follow your brothers like a dog."

As Tora grew weaker, she said she craved nature, the warm air on her skin, the dappled shade, the murmur of the stream and the sounds of birds and insects, the night sky and the stars. Delivering the children had made her gentle, as though her hardness and fire had all drained into them.

At her request, Shisoku took a clear amber jewel from the altar and placed it on her chest. Shika carried her outside, where she lay for several days, neither eating nor drinking, but seemingly at peace. The children played around her, growing visibly every day.

"How did you escape from Matsutani?" Shika asked, one morning. "We all thought you died in the fire."

"I will burn," she replied, "but then was not the right time. I realized what Kiyoyori's wife might do; I would have done the same, or worse. I left then, but a part of myself—we call it the second self—remained behind long enough to fool anyone watching and make them believe I was still inside. I came to Shisoku, my mission complete. I had the gift of five men within me: the sorcerer, the bandit, the sage, the warrior, and the youth who is or will be all these things—as will be my sons, my little tribe. I did not know that you would return, but, now you have, I see I can entrust them to you."

"Which one is mine?" Shika asked. They both turned their eyes to them.

"They are all mingled, so they are all yours. They're beautiful, don't you think? I am glad I chose handsome men like you and Kiyoyori."

Shika saw how her face and voice changed as she spoke his name.

"What will happen to the lord's spirit?" he said.

"I don't know. When is it time for the foal to be born? Unless you can find your horses again, we will never know." After a moment she said, "I really loved Kiyoyori—in the way you people love each other, and we, not so much. I had never felt that before. I should be able to pass away without regret, as easily as the leaf falls from the tree in autumn, but the idea of never seeing him again, in whatever form, fills me with sorrow. I cling to life for his sake. This is what love does to you, Shikanoko. See how the false wolf grows more real every day, because it has become attached to you. It shivers at your approach and wags its tail at the sound of your voice. It has made you its master, it lives for your affection. But, as your saints teach and we have always known, attachment enslaves you. Only those free from it see the world as it really is and have power over themselves and all things."

"I will never have that," he said in a low voice. "I cannot forget Akihime. I am tormented by love for her and terrible remorse that I betrayed her. I feel I must leave this place and search for her and Yoshimori. I have vowed to restore him to the Lotus Throne. How can I do that if I have to care for five children?"

Tora had closed her eyes and turned her face to the sun. She spoke so quietly he had to bend closer to hear her.

"Be patient. Teach the children how to be human, so they can pass in the world. Look after them well. When they are grown, they will help you in your quest."

He thought her breathing stopped then, but he could not be sure. He felt heat glow from her and saw the rays of the sun had hit the jewel on her chest and ignited her robe. The children stopped their play and stood around, staring with their expressionless eyes. The flames grew quickly and in a moment had engulfed her, as though she were no more than dried grass. Nothing remained of her, no skull or bones, just the ash that Shisoku gathered up and placed in a carved box in front of the altar. The boys did not seem to miss her or to grieve, and even Shika, who had grieved so much, did not know how to teach them.

Shisoku took the blood and other fluids from childbirth and spread them over the two broken halves of the mask. He bound the pieces together with what was left of the strands of the cocoons. They covered the face like a spider's web, silver and gray against the lacquer. He said many spells to protect it anew and placed it on the altar. When Shika knelt before it he thought he could hear tiny sounds as the edges knitted together, as had the bones in his arm.

Next Shisoku turned his attention to the ruined sword. Despite the heat, he built up the fire until the embers glowed white. He sent the boys, who were now the size of five-year-olds, out into the forest to the warm, sandy spots where snakes shed their skins. They found several dry, papery patterned skins, and Kuro, who already showed an affinity with all poisonous creatures, brought back a live adder. Shisoku showed him how to hold its head and milk its venom. The skins were added to the fire, and the venom to the molten steel.

Shisoku killed the adder and skinned it carefully, putting the skin aside to bind the hilt, after the scorched mother-of-pearl had been removed. The steel was hammered and folded over and again, cooled in the clear mountain water, reheated, cooled again. Mu in particular was fascinated by the process and followed every step closely.

The essence of the snake was absorbed into the blade and Shisoku named it Jato, the snake sword. He would not let Shika touch it, but placed it outside in the cleft of two rocks. He tied a white straw rope around the rocks.

"The elements must temper it," he said. "And we must let it choose whether or not to come to your hand."

None of the boys spoke much although they understood everything that was said to them. They were thin, with slender limbs, and were always hungry, eating voraciously to fuel their rapid growth. Their favorite food was meat, and Shika went hunting every day to bring back rabbits and squirrels, sometimes wild boar, though he never killed deer. The skins were cleaned and dried to make winter clothes, but in the heat of late summer the boys went naked. They fought all the time, testing one another's strength and agility and endurance of pain, but at night they slept in a tumbled heap, like puppies.

One evening Shika saw Kiku seem to divide into two people, spontaneously, as though he had no idea what he was doing. He realized it was the second self that Lady Tora had told him about. Almost at the same time, Mu vanished from his sight and reappeared a few moments later on the other side of the stream. These abilities were innate; he could teach them nothing about them, nor could Shisoku. Instead both shared their own particular skills.

Shika fashioned poles and instructed them in the basic moves of sword fighting. He made small bows and showed them how to shape arrows. They trapped birds and collected the feathers for the fletches, and learned how to string and draw a bow.

Shisoku demonstrated how to forge sharp knives and other weapons, and he taught them all the poisons that could be found in the forest, as well as the snakes, aconite and bryony, the kernels of certain nuts, toadstools and other fungi.

Ku, as his mother had predicted, loved the animals, the fake ones as much as the real, but Kiku and Kuro were indifferent to them, though they teased the false ones mercilessly, tripping up the water carriers, jumping out at the guard dogs. The real animals snapped at them, but the false ones never did. They had been created without aggression. But one day Kiku came bleeding from a wound on the cheek.

"Your wolf bit me." It was the longest sentence Shika had ever heard from him.

He cleaned the bite, saying, "That will teach you to leave him alone." He realized he had spoken of the wolf as *him*, as though it were truly alive. Tora had said it was love that made the wolf become more real, but *he* had also become aggressive in a way the other false animals were not. Now that the wolf was truly alive he seemed to need a name, and Shika decided to call him Gen, which might mean either Reality or Illusion.

Shisoku had still not given permission for Shika to touch the sword Jato when, in the eighth month, a typhoon swept up from the southwest. The wind tore trees up by the roots and threw them down. Rain fell from the sky like a river. The stream roared through the night and raged across the clearing. Many of the false animals were swept away, their empty skins caught on tree branches, their skulls washed up on the bank miles away.

At the height of the storm, Shisoku said, "Jato is outside."

Shika went out. The wind seized him and shook him. A false dog flew past his head and crashed into a tree. He could see the rock where Jato lay, but it was already almost submerged. He thought he saw the sword gleam beneath the rushing water and struggled toward it, fighting the wind, but the current dragged it loose. It disappeared with a flash of steel, a water snake in the flood.

When the wind and the rain abated, and the stream

returned to its normal size, Shika and the boys searched the valley, but the sword had vanished.

"It must be buried in mud and silt," he said to Shisoku after another day of fruitless searching.

"When it wants to be found it will be," Shisoku replied.

It made Shika sad and angry. He had called Kiyoyori's spirit back from the gates of Hell, he had rescued the ruined sword. Now both had vanished into the Darkwood, as if they had not thought him worthy of them.

At the end of the ninth month, Shisoku pronounced the mask healed. Although it was not perfect as it had been and one antler remained broken, it had different powers, attained through suffering and loss. Shika put it away in the seven-layered brocade bag, reluctant to face the Prince Abbot as he knew one day he must, and, in the calm autumn days, began to work at the fire, helped by Shisoku and Mu. They forged a new sword and called it Jinan, Second Son, and a helmet mounted with iron antlers, one broken in the same way as the mask's, and armor, bound with leather lacing, dyed with madder and indigo. It seemed there was nothing Shisoku did not have stored away somewhere, and what was not stored he could find in the forest.

"Are you planning to go to war with someone?" he asked Shika when the armor was finished.

"With my uncle first. The boys cannot just grow up in the forest. They need a home, they need learning, far more than I can teach them. I am going to take back Kumayama. After that who knows? Maybe Kuromori and Matsutani. Maybe I will be like Akuzenji, become a bandit and control

trade as King of the Mountain. Then I will be able to pro-
vide for the boys."

"They are not ordinary boys," Shisoku said dubiously.
"You are not going to be able to turn them into warriors."

"Maybe not. I will turn them into something very useful to myself, though," said Shikanoko. "I suppose I'll need
a bow, too."

"I will make you one," the sorcerer promised. "Do you
remember what Ameyumi looked like?"

"Only that it was enormous and no one could draw it
but my father."

But it seemed Shikanoko remembered more than he
thought, or Shisoku somehow drew the knowledge from
hidden memories. When the bow was finished, it felt the
way his father's bow had, in his hand. They named it
Kodama: Echo.

"Will Ameyumi ever be found?" he wondered aloud.

"It will, but not by you," replied the mountain sorcerer.

2

MASACHIKA

Masachika opened his eyes on the familiar setting of his boyhood home—*opened*, he thought, was not quite the correct word, as he could barely see through the swelling. His skin burned and itched and beneath the inflammation he ached from head to foot. His tongue was swollen and his lips cracked.

He realized where he was from the outline of the mountains beyond the one open shutter—the rest were closed and barred on the inside. It was raining steadily, but even the dull light of a wet day and overcast sky was too bright, sending a piercing pain deep into the back of his skull. He closed his eyes and tried to ask for water.

"He is awake," a woman's voice said. He thought he knew it from his childhood. "Go and tell Hironaga."

Hironaga, he knew, was this woman's husband. Had they not been as close to him as foster parents? Was he a boy again, had he fallen from his horse? He could remember nothing.

"What happened?" he muttered. He did not really care about the answer. He was sure he was dying. A pitiful rage flickered within him; it was too soon, he did not want to leave yet, if only he could stay. But living entailed so much pain. Maybe it was better to slip away into the numbness of death.

The woman held a cup to his lips and he gulped down the lukewarm, slightly salty liquid. It only partly quenched his thirst. His gullet burned and smarted.

He heard footsteps and a man knelt at his side.

"Lord Masachika? Can you hear me?"

The woman had taken away the cup and was bathing his face. The cloth felt cool and soothing. He nodded and felt it slide against his skin. Then it, too, was removed. He could see a little better. Hironaga, a man in his fifties with graying hair and a weathered face, was bending over him.

"We found you after the attack. We were searching the hillside for spent arrows and uninjured horses. Luckily, it was I who came across you and I recognized you. You have been unconscious for a long time. My wife has been caring for you—you know she always loved you like her own son."

"The attack?" He half-recalled the desperate plunge down the hillside.

"We knew it was coming. Young Chikamaru, Kongyo's son, came from Matsutani to warn us. The Miboshi horsemen plunged straight into a trap. None of them survived. If you had not fallen from your horse halfway down, you would have been killed, too. We could see very little in the dark and we would never have known who you were."

He remembered that he was Miboshi now. Didn't Hironaga know that? He frowned, confused, and pain shot around his eyeballs.

While his eyes were shut he thought he sensed someone else approaching. Again he knew the voice.

"Lord Masachika," it said.

He peered through swollen eyelids.

"It is I, Kongyo. Do you remember me?"

He nodded. "You were my brother's friend."

"I became his senior retainer, and will be yours, too, I hope. We all know how your father commanded you to go to the Miboshi. You cannot be blamed for obeying him. But something prevented you from attacking your family home. If your brother, Kiyoyori, and his only son are indeed dead, then you are the last of the Kuromori lords. Your father made a difficult decision to preserve his family line. Who are we to put an end to it? Heaven spared you. We could not go against its judgment."

"I feel more like Heaven punished me," Masachika said and groaned.

"Heaven gives punishment with one hand and mercy with the other," Hironaga said.

Masachika remembered how the older man had always been inclined to make these sanctimonious pronouncements. At that moment he realized two things. One was that despite the pain he would rather be alive than dead; the other, that he was going to be given another chance.

He closed his eyes again and began to prepare himself to take full advantage of it.

※

It was a tiny fortress, not quite under siege, but anticipating another attack any day. The men, almost forty in number, were bored and tense, and always hungry. They waited for news, of a Kakizuki counterattack or confirmation of Lord Kiyoyori's death, but none came. The bodies of the dead Miboshi had been burned, their swords, bows, and arrows added to the armory. No one came to avenge them or to punish the Kuromori group.

It rained frequently. The summer days were lush and humid. Farmers paraded outside with food—eggs, summer greens and other vegetables—and every day a handful of men climbed the hill behind the fortress to hunt rabbits and deer.

The farmers reported that the spirits were still in residence at Matsutani, and no one dared go inside the garden walls. Weeds were growing rampant in the rains and the house was disappearing beneath them.

Masachika had many long hours in which to reflect on what the future held for him. As the swelling in his face slowly went down his memory came back, but the bee stings left aftereffects, fierce headaches and night fevers. He dreaded confronting the spirits again, yet he became obsessed with ousting them. The idea of Matsutani rotting away, after all the sacrifices that had been made, gnawed at him constantly. He could not help thinking of Tama. He was sorry he had hired the assassin. It had been an impulsive act and he regretted it. He didn't even know if the man had been successful; he had not had time to find out before he left with the Miboshi army. But to be on the safe side he offered prayers for her soul in the makeshift shrine that had been erected inside the fortress.

Hironaga and Kongyo, with their simple concepts of lineage and loyalty, seemed to assume he had returned not only to Kuromori but also to the Kakizuki. Of course he had not; he had a better idea of how things were in the capital. He knew who the real victors were. He was not going to join the losers' side at this stage of the war. But it was not hard to pretend his new retainers were right, nor to agree with them that what they most needed was information, and that he was perfectly placed to get it for them.

He made a convincing show of gratitude to Hironaga, respect for Kongyo, affection for his old foster mother, joy at being back in his childhood home. Just as he had in Minatogura, he endeared himself to most of the men, already predisposed to accept him as their departed lord's brother, by undertaking any task alongside them, willingly and competently, by remembering their names, their characteristics, and their exploits.

"Could you get to Lord Keita, who, it seems, has retreated with the Kakizuki forces to Rakuhara?" Kongyo asked him one morning. It promised to be the first clear day for several weeks. The plum rains were drawing to an end.

"I can certainly return to the capital. I served the Miboshi well during the years I lived with them. I believe they trust me well enough. I could assess the situation there and report to Lord Keita, get a message back to you or return myself."

"Ask him if we should remain here or fight our way through to join him," Hironaga said.

One of the men who was listening spoke up. "Lord Masachika was with the Miboshi for eight years and was part of the force that attacked us. Forgive me, but someone has to say it. Can we really trust him?"

"Tsunesada," Masachika replied, "a man cannot forget his first loyalties. I longed to return to my true family, especially since my revered brother appears to have passed on to the next world. I was born Kakizuki and Heaven has decreed I should become Kakizuki again."

"Even though the Miboshi rule the capital and the Kakizuki are in exile?" Tsunesada persisted.

"That makes my choice all the more honorable," Masachika said smoothly.

Tsunesada pointed at the stack of reports that Masachika had written and that had been retrieved from the saddlebags of his fallen horse. They had sat for weeks on the floor of the room in which the men were now gathered, because no one could decipher them. "What do all these mean?"

"They are records of the warriors. The men dictated them to me because I can read and write."

"Not much use now they are all dead!" Tsunesada scoffed.

"The records give them immortality. Their names live on. If I take them with me, they will be sent to Minatogura and their families may be able to claim compensation."

Hironaga was frowning. "Do the Miboshi do the same in everything?"

"Keep records? They do. It is Lord Aritomo's method to know everything, remember everything, control everything. Memory cannot be trusted. Five men will remember the same event in five different ways, but written accounts become legal records. Aritomo loves legality."

The men shuffled uneasily.

"If I present them in the capital I can make myself seem more credible," Masachika said, "but burn them if you like."

Tsunesada looked at Kongyo. The older man said, "I suppose Masachika is right. He had better take them with him."

A few days later, supplied with a new horse and his own sword, Masachika slipped away from Kuromori before dawn and rode toward Shimaura. But he did not follow the western coast road to the capital. Instead he turned east to Minatogura. He had been thinking about this plan for weeks and had decided he must confirm his legal claim on Matsutani. Only then would he return to Miyako.

Compared with the half-destroyed capital, Minatogura looked peaceful and prosperous, hardly touched by war. Its ships sailed to and from the port, laden with goods that its wealthy merchants bought and sold with even more vigor than usual. The news of the Miboshi victory and the Kakizuki defeat had given the city an atmosphere of triumph.

In offices and courts, scribes and lawyers recorded these victories, and the exploits of individual warriors, and calculated the rewards in land that would be granted, and from whom, among the defeated, such lands would be taken.

Masachika went to his adoptive family's house, riding through the familiar streets, past the port and up the slope to the north. It was very hot, the sun was blinding in a brilliant sky, yet shivers ran through him and his head ached. He was aware that, unless the onset of war had delayed it, his claim would have been decided. He told himself there was nothing to be nervous about—the estate could be granted only to him; there were no other heirs; he had served the Miboshi faithfully—yet his anxiety persisted. What if he had been ruled dead, or worse, a traitor? Only legal confirmation that Matsutani was his would bring him reassurance and tranquility.

His adoptive father, Yamada Keisaku, came hurrying out to the gate as Masachika dismounted and handed the horse's reins to a groom.

"You are home, and safe! We heard rumors that you had been killed in an attack on Kuromori. Heaven be praised! My wife has prayed for you day and night, and our daughter—how she has wept, believing you dead and our family bereaved."

Masachika brushed aside his effusive welcome. Keisaku was a pious and jovial man who wanted everyone around him to be happy, but Masachika had never had much respect for him, despising his excessive religious faith and what he considered shallowness.

Inside the house he caught a glimpse of his betrothed, her plump pretty face flushed with excitement and joy, her eyes all the more sparkling for her tears. He pretended not to see her.

"Is there any news from the tribunal?" he asked immediately.

"About your claim?" Keisaku replied. "We want you to know you will always be our son. We have a country estate, more remote and not as wealthy as Matsutani, of course, but which will always be yours. You will never be landless."

"What are you talking about?" Masachika demanded.

Keisaku was rubbing his hands together nervously. "I am grieved to be the one to reveal such disappointing news. Despite my deep affection for you I am the one who must inflict a grave wound. Accept it as Heaven's will for your life. No doubt good will come of it in the end."

"Are you trying to tell me my claim has failed?" Masachika said, incredulous.

"Your former wife, Lady Tama, produced documents that stated clearly the land was left by her father to her and whoever was her husband—Matsutani, that is. No ruling was made on Kuromori, which I suppose would still be yours."

Masachika stared at his adoptive father, speechless. So Hisoku had failed. Tama was not only alive but had dared to approach the tribunal in her own right. He was outraged and furious, but at the same time he couldn't help admiring her audacity, and he felt the stirrings of old longing.

Oblivious to his future son-in-law's inner turmoil, Keisaku said, "Lady Tama has a powerful ally in the Abbess at Muenji . . . however, the reasons are not important; the court found in her favor."

"But she is a woman!" Masachika could think of nothing else to say.

"As the only surviving child of her father, and the widow of the Kuromori lord, she was considered to hold the greater right," Keisaku said. "As the father of an only daughter, I have some sympathy with this judgment."

"Surely I have a chance to appeal? I would have been here pleading my own case if I had not been fighting for the Miboshi, and nearly dying, I might add!"

"I cannot answer you on that subject. You could try speaking to someone of higher rank. Yukikuni no Takaakira, for example; he is here in Minatogura for a few days. Our meager estate borders his, so I have some channels through which to approach him."

"Takaakira? He has taken over Kiyoyori's old house in Miyako."

"That is good." Keisaku attempted a smile. "He will consider himself beholden to you."

"Do you think so? If a man wrongs you once, he will find it easier the next time. I can't expect much help from him."

"My dear son, you must not be so cynical. I will do my best with him. Meanwhile, let us put our trust in the Enlightened One and bear whatever Heaven sends us."

Masachika could not hide his irritation, thinking,

What Heaven sends is one thing, but to bear the platitudes of the old is quite another.

He tried to see Tama, but when he went to Muenji he was refused admittance. He was told the lady was practicing a religious retreat.

"For how long?" he demanded.

"It is hard to say."

"Will she see me if I come back in a few days?"

"It is hard to say."

That was the only answer he received.

His adoptive father began to make delicate attempts to contact Yukikuni no Takaakira while Masachika waited impatiently, avoiding his betrothed and her mother and putting off any discussion of marriage. Tama had suddenly become desirable to him once more. He recalled the early days of their marriage, her ardor and eagerness, his terrible pain when she had been taken from him. He convinced himself that she was still his wife. Had she not made it clear she wanted him back last time they met? This time he would not refuse her.

Even the nagging memory of the spirits did not discourage him. He would face them again with Tama, whom they had called the Matsutani lady, by his side. Together they would find a way to placate or remove them.

Four days later he was told a messenger was at the door. He rushed out and immediately recognized Hisoku, the rogue he had hired.

"Lady Tama wishes to see you before she leaves," Hisoku said.

"Where is she going?" Masachika could not hide his surprise.

Hisoku met his gaze insolently. "We are leaving tomorrow for Matsutani."

"We?" The word shocked him. He could not bring himself to believe all its implications.

"Lady Tama has graciously taken me into her service."

"She will soon find out how incompetent you are," Masachika said with scorn.

Hisoku did not reply, but Masachika saw a muscle twitch in his cheek. It did not worry him that he had made an enemy. He despised the man and had already decided he would kill him at the first opportunity.

However, he had to follow him to the temple, where they were taken to the garden pavilion. Even here in the shade by the lake, where water trickled from the spring, it was unbearably hot. Cicadas droned deafeningly from the woods.

Masachika went forward, leaving Hisoku waiting on the step. He studied his former wife with respect. She seemed both unaffected by the heat and possessed of a new, calm authority.

"Your religious retreat has been beneficial," he observed.

She did not respond to his trace of sarcasm, simply indicating that he might sit next to her.

"You desired to see me?" she said.

"Tama," he began.

"Lady Tama," Hisoku corrected him.

"Can we speak in private?" Masachika tried to mask his impatience.

"How can I be sure you will not make another attempt on my life?" Tama replied.

"That was a mistake, I apologize . . ." His excuses trailed away under her level gaze. "Forgive me," he said simply.

Without turning her head, she said, "You may wait a little farther away, Hisoku."

The man moved a few paces to the edge of the lake, but did not take his eyes off them.

"What do you want, Masachika?" Tama said.

"I want us to live together as husband and wife."

She continued to look at him without speaking and a slight smile began to curve her lips.

"You will agree?" he said eagerly. "I may come with you to Matsutani?"

Now her eyes were alight with emotion. He leaned forward to take her in his arms, but in one swift movement she was on her feet.

"It is too late."

Then she was gone, hurrying down the path by the side of the lake.

"What?" he shouted after her. "You won't even listen to me?"

"I think Lady Tama has made her feelings clear," Hisoku said, giving Masachika a triumphant, sneering look before he followed her.

Two days later, still burning with regret and rage, Masachika found himself in the presence of Yukikuni no Takaakira. He did not want to be there, he would have preferred to leave meeting Takaakira until he returned to Miyako, but his father-in-law had gone to great efforts to obtain the audience, eager for Masachika to seek support for his appeal. However, Takaakira was not inclined to help him or even to listen to him. He cut short Masachika's explanation, saying, "That has no interest for me. What does interest me is Kuromori."

"My lord?"

"You left with a hundred men. All of them, save Yasuie, appear to be dead. The fortress is still in the hands of your late brother's retainers, yet you have not only survived but were permitted to leave. What deal did you strike with them and whose side are you on now?"

His voice was deliberately insulting. Masachika knew Takaakira could be both charming and generous to those he respected, and it wounded him to realize he was not one of them. He began to defend himself.

"I am, and for years have been, Miboshi. Does your lordship not recall how well I acquitted myself at Shimaura and the Sagigawa?" It did not seem to be the time for false modesty. "I deeply regret the failure at Kuromori, but I was attacked by evil spirits and rendered unconscious before the actual battle."

The mention of the spirits, he could see, aroused Takaakira's interest, and he found himself relating the strange occurrences at Matsutani, Yasunobu's death, and the crippling bee stings. Takaakira heard him out and then said,

"That is one of the most fanciful explanations for a defeat I have ever had to listen to. So, you did not agree to spy for the Kakizuki, and to try to get to Keita in Rakuhara?"

Again Masachika felt the flick of contempt. He hid his anger and affected a penitent air. "I can hide nothing from such a great and wise lord. I did agree, but only so I could escape and return to Lord Aritomo's service. I have even brought with me the records of the warriors who died. The men at Kuromori trust me and regard me as Kiyoyori's heir. Surely that can be turned to our advantage?"

"Kuromori will have to be dealt with eventually," Takaakira said. "In the meantime I have a task for you. I do want you to go to Rakuhara. Everyone suspects you of spying for the Kakizuki, so you will return to them, but you will be spying for us. Now you have lost your inheritance it will be a consolation for you."

When Masachika did not answer, Takaakira went on, "I am doing this for Keisaku's sake, since we are neighbors. I know you do not lack courage, Masachika. I have seen you in battle. But you have a self-serving nature that makes you untrustworthy. This is your chance to redeem yourself. If you refuse, Lord Aritomo will require you to take your own life in compensation for your failure, and to wipe out the suspicions that are growing around you."

"I will do whatever you and Lord Aritomo command," Masachika said, prostrating himself. But beneath his feigned humility his mind was searching desperately for some new strategy that might improve his position.

"Good. You will leave tomorrow. That will be all."

Takaakira gave a brief nod and turned away, but Masachika did not want the interview to end on such unequal terms, nor did he like the idea of his life and future held in the other man's hands.

"May I ask one question?" he said, as he sat up.

The lord gave his permission with another slight nod.

He was playing for time, not even sure what question he was going to ask, when an image of the house in the capital came into his mind and he made one of his intuitive stabs in the dark.

"I believe your lordship has taken over Kiyoyori's old house in the capital." He felt Takaakira's flash of surprise and anger and knew he had hit on something. "Don't misunderstand me; it is an honor for our family. But was his daughter there? Did she survive?"

"I did not know whose the house was, or even that Kiyoyori had a daughter. The place was empty," Takaakira replied. "That's all I can tell you."

But something in his face told Masachika that the noble lord of the Snow Country was lying.

3

AKI

When Shikanoko left, Aki lay rigid with shock, tears pooling in her eyes and spilling over her cheeks. She could never become a shrine maiden now, never undo what they had done. She was filled with regret and fear—surely the gods would punish them? After a while she picked up the catalpa bow and went to the stream to wash herself, her blood disappearing into the cold water. She was shivering, not only from the chill but also from emotions she did not recognize. She blamed herself as much as him. The world was colorless, leached of enchantment and mystery. Yet there had been both earlier, something had taken place, some spell had been cast over them, girl and boy, that neither had been able to resist.

I could have fought him off, she thought, as the water flowed over her, *I could have killed him. Why didn't I?* And she answered herself, *Because I wanted to touch his skin, place my mouth on his, be held by him and hold him, and I have done so ever since I saw him, when those men lay dead, killed by his arrows. But I did not know it would be like that, so brutal, so painful. And now I have done exactly what my father told me not to do. It can never be undone. I am another person now.*

Like a wild animal, she longed to flee into the forest. Then she thought of killing herself, but she had left her knife in the hut; and she could not leave Yoshi. While he lived she must live, too.

It began to rain. Not wanting to return to the hut, yet needing to think clearly, she stood up, pulled her robe around her, and walked to the cave, where the horses were tied up on long lines.

Nyorin was standing, and whinnied softly at her approach. Risu was lying down, and did not want to get up. They must have been restless during the night, for they had stepped over the loose ropes several times and had entangled themselves. She untied them and pulled the ropes free. Then she lay down next to the mare, within the cradle of her legs, and rested her head on her belly. She imagined she could hear the foal's heartbeat. Could the spirit of Lord Kiyoyori really have taken possession of it? She remembered him from the few times she had seen him, his courageous bearing, his imposing looks. How pitiful his fate had been. Tears formed in her eyes. She could hear the soft dripping from the rocks and trees around the cave, a gentle, soothing sound. Nyorin stamped. Risu whickered.

Her mind began to drift. Suddenly she was dreaming

of monkeys. She awoke to hear someone calling her name.

"Akihime!"

Nyorin neighed loudly and Risu began to struggle to her feet.

He called again. "Akihime!"

She did not want to go out to him. How could she meet his gaze? She shrank back for a moment, listening to the dawn's birdsong, the constant dripping of the rain, the babble of the stream. Yet she wanted to see him; almost against her will, her feet led her outside, the bow gripped in her hand.

She saw the masked figure come from the hut with Yoshimori. It looked like a being from a dream or from the distant magical past. The antlers gave it height and authority, and it moved in a way that was neither human nor animal but that exuded force and power.

Hardly believing her eyes, she saw the kneeling boy, the drawn sword, as if they were part of the dream. For a few moments she stood without moving, the horses, as motionless, beside her, their ears pricked forward, their eyes startled. Then she raised the catalpa bow and twanged it, she heard the scream of the werehawk, and, as if the sound of the bow released them, the horses bolted from the cave, Risu in the lead.

Aki ran after them, and watched as they attacked Shikanoko.

She thought they had killed him. Sobbing with grief and shock and fury, she ran to Yoshi and held him close against her. Kon fluttered around her head, saying something she did not understand. Yoshi clung to her, trembling. He muttered something.

Aki bent down. "What?"

"I was brave, wasn't I?"

"You were very brave," she said.

"Was Shikanoko going to cut my head off?"

"Yes!" she screamed, then tried, for the boy's sake, to control herself.

"Why? I thought he was going to protect us."

"I thought so, too. But he is in the service of a very powerful man who wants to kill you. Shikanoko has to obey him."

"I liked him," Yoshi said, sadness in his eyes.

"Like, *like*? What does that mean?" Aki replied. It was far too tame a word. "Luckily, some other force is looking after you. Heaven itself is protecting you. But we must get away from this place."

"And leave him here?"

Shikanoko's eyelids fluttered briefly and he cried out in pain but did not wake. Yoshi looked down on him. "Shouldn't we take care of him?"

"He was going to kill you," Aki said. "He will try again."

"We should love our enemies," Yoshi said stubbornly.

"Where did you get that idea from?" Aki was wondering if she should finish Shikanoko off before he regained consciousness.

"I heard the old man on the boat tell the musicians. I liked it."

"I remember him," Aki said. It seemed like something from a different world.

"I don't want anyone else to die." Yoshi was close to tears.

"Come," she said gently. "We are going to get away before he wakes; we will leave him to Heaven. Fetch Genzo and my knife while I get the horses ready."

He nodded, gave one more worried look at Shikanoko, and went to the hut, the werehawk fluttering after him. It had more gold feathers than ever, Aki noticed. They gleamed through the misty rain.

The horses, calm now, lowered their heads to their unconscious master and drew in his smell. Then they followed Aki docilely to the cave and stood while she fumbled with the saddle and bridles. When Yoshi returned, she put the knife in her belt and tied the lute on her back. Was that the faintest echo of the love song?

"Traitor," she said to it silently. "I should burn you!"

She lifted Yoshi onto Risu's back.

"You don't have to hold the reins. I'll knot them on her neck and lead you."

"I can ride," he said. "Anyway, Risu won't let anything bad happen to me."

Aki was surprised he knew the mare's name. "What's the stallion called?"

"Nyorin. It means Silver. And the werehawk's name is Kon—Gold. That's funny, isn't it? Silver and Gold."

"Do you listen to everything, and remember it?" she asked.

He nodded. "I understand it, mostly, though sometimes not till later, after I've thought about it for a while."

He will be a fine emperor, Aki said to herself. *And he will have seen life in a way no other emperor has.*

"Where are we going now?" Yoshi said, as she scrambled up onto Nyorin's back. The stallion was much taller than the mare, but he waited patiently, and let her settle in the saddle and take up the reins, before he moved off.

"I'm not sure." Aki was trying to form a plan. They had the horses, the werehawk—if it, too, did not betray them and fly back to Ryusonji—and the untrustworthy lute. She had her knife and the catalpa bow, and she knew a little about the herbs and seeds of the forest. But they could not hide out there forever, not in winter, though that was still half a year away. She decided to ride north, keeping away from the roads, to Rinrakuji, as her father had told her to. Maybe someone who could help them had survived there. If not, she would go on to Kitakami and from there down the Kitagawa and the western side of the lake to Nishimi.

"I will show you where I lived when I was a little girl," she told Yoshi. Nishimi was closer to where the Kakizuki were in exile. There she would find the men and the arms Yoshi was going to need.

She explained this out loud, as though she expected the werehawk and the horses to understand it, and let Nyorin have his head. He immediately set out up the valley to the east. She thought they should be heading north, but the valley grew narrower and the forest thicker; east was the only direction possible unless they turned back. But the fear of finding Shikanoko dead made that impossible.

After a couple of hours the rain stopped. The sun had

climbed high in the sky and now its rays pierced the clouds. It became very hot, the earth steaming around them. The horses stopped in a grassy clearing where the mountain stream had formed pools filled with bulrushes and lotus stems. They drank deeply and then began to tear at the long grass.

"It looks like we're taking a rest," Aki said. She slid down from Nyorin's back, flinching at the pain, noticing she had left smears of blood on his silver coat, and helped Yoshi dismount. A dove was calling from the forest and she could hear the pretty whistle of something she thought might be a grosbeak, though she knew it only from poetry.

Yoshi said, "Older sister, what are we going to eat?"

"Good question," Aki said. "We could always eat grass like Risu and Nyorin."

Yoshi pulled up a few blades, crammed them in his mouth, chewed bravely for a few moments, then spat them out.

"No? I'll have to see what else I can find. You rest here, under that tree. Keep an eye on the horses. Don't let them stray out of sight. And look after Genzo."

She waded into one of the pools and pulled up the rushes, throwing them to the bank behind her. The mud was cool and soothing to her feet. Little fishes darted away through the tawny water, but she had nothing to catch them with. Farther up the stream, she saw a flash of gold and Kon flew up with a loud squawk, a small sweetfish in his talons.

"Take it to Yoshi," she called, but Kon was already flying back to the tree. It returned and took another fish from the water. Aki felt her stomach ache at the thought of food. How long was it since they had eaten? She could not remember.

She cut the succulent roots from the rushes and chewed on one. The grosbeak sang again and this time she saw it, gray and black, flying to a rock in the stream. A wagtail answered, and then above the birdsong came music. Genzo was playing, the same love song from the previous night, awakening the longing and the fear she had been trying to forget.

"I will smash that lute," she cried, "heirloom or not!"

She ran back to the tree where Yoshi sat cross-legged. Kon was tearing pieces off the fish and feeding him like a baby bird. The lute's decoration sparkled in the sun as the music poured from it.

And around them in a half circle, just like in her dream, sat ten or more gray-furred, rosy-faced, green-eyed monkeys.

Aki stood still. She had never been so close to wild monkeys and she was uncertain how they would behave. She did not want to be attacked by them nor did she want to scare them away. Was it the lute that enchanted them, or Yoshi? Did they recognize him in some way as the divine Emperor? Of course, she reasoned to herself, they should, all creatures should, since the true emperor was the link between Heaven and earth. It was his prayers and rituals that kept both in balance and harmony, affecting the well-being of monkeys as much as men.

A usurper on the throne would cause disasters and catastrophes, earthquakes, plagues, fires, and floods. Maybe these were already occurring in the capital. She had no way of knowing. The forest was so peaceful, the birds singing, the grass lush and bright with wildflowers.

Yoshi saw her and called out, "Look, older sister! Monkeys!"

She remembered he had called that out once before, at the island market at Majima, by the Rainbow Bridge, when he had seen the boy he had so much admired and his monkey friends. And she had dreamed of monkeys. Was it a sign that fate had brought them together for some purpose?

In the middle of the semicircle a large female sat nursing a baby. Something about her suggested authority, and Aki approached her with deference. Genzo stopped playing and the monkeys all turned their heads and chattered softly. Aki fell to her knees as she would to a court lady, or the Crown Princess herself, held out the catalpa bow and laid it down, and bowed to the ground. The monkey matriarch put out a hand and gently scratched the girl's head, put her fingers to her nose and sniffed them, then shuffled a little closer, shifting the baby to the other nipple, and began to run her fingers through Aki's cropped hair, searching for fleas, grooming her.

Aki submitted without moving and felt some deep, wordless connection with the old monkey: acceptance, the assurance of protection and support. Tears formed in her eyes suddenly. Somehow under the gentle fingers she went from a kneeling position to lying down. She could hear the horses tearing at the grass. Through the foliage the sun cast leafy patterns on her closed eyelids. The monkeys chattered to one another. Yoshi laughed. Kon called in response, almost tunefully.

The day passed, and at dusk they followed the monkeys to a place where hot water bubbled up into rock-edged pools. Here the monkeys lived. Yoshi wanted nothing more than to stay with them, and Aki could not refuse him.

4

TAKAAKIRA

Takaakira had kept the girl hidden in her old home in the capital for several months. When he returned from Minatogura, he had made more searching enquiries and found the house had indeed been the residence of Kiyoyori's family, as he had learned from Masachika. The girl must be Kiyoyori's daughter.

The realization made him both angry and surprised at himself. He prided himself on knowing all the secrets of the city; how could he not have seen what was in front of his eyes? Kiyoyori might have been only a provincial warrior, but his unwavering support of the Crown Prince, his noble death, the mysterious death of his son, and the legends that were growing up around them ensured his name was still very much alive. The Prince Abbot, who had grown even more powerful now he was uncle to the Emperor, hated Kiyoyori, even more in death than in life.

Takaakira had told Masachika that the house was empty,

but when he recalled the other man's expression it made him uneasy. He did not want to give Masachika any influence over him. He was the girl's uncle, after all. What was to prevent him turning up at his former home and discovering her? Would he recognize her? Did she resemble her father? Why had he suddenly asked about the house? Had something made him suspect that Kiyoyori's daughter had survived? The risk of being betrayed by Masachika, or anyone else, began to disturb him. He must either hide her somewhere else or kill her himself. If she were discovered, she would be tortured and put to death and he—he could not imagine what punishment Lord Aritomo would devise for him.

He knew he could never bring himself to end her life. Every day she delighted him more with her intelligence and wit, and her beauty, on the cusp of womanhood. He loved her like a daughter, but he dreamed of holding her in his arms as his wife. She seemed to adore him; she sought to please him, she learned rapidly. When he was away, the servants told him, she spent her time studying, fretting for his return. By the end of summer she was reading fluently. He brought scrolls for her from his own library in Minatogura, works of literature and history, essays and poems. She grasped the essentials of poetry swiftly and began writing poems every day for him.

He educated her taste in clothes, colors and materials. He taught her to discern incense and perfume, he played music and demonstrated dance steps, found women to instruct her and moved them into his household.

She was a consolation to him during a difficult time.

The city was hit by a series of disasters. A fire broke out in the sixth month and destroyed most of the newly completed buildings. An epidemic of sickness raged for weeks, leaving thousands dead. Smoke from funeral pyres darkened the skies and many of those who survived succumbed to starvation as the rains came for three weeks and then dried up. Rice crops failed, beans withered on the stem, fruit did not ripen. The new emperor offered prayers for rain and as if in mockery Heaven sent a ferocious typhoon that swept across the country, flooding rivers and washing away bridges. Water ran waist-deep through the streets of the capital, gravid with the bodies of the drowned.

People began to say openly that Heaven was outraged, that they were being punished for the crimes of their rulers. These mutterings eventually reached the ears of Lord Aritomo, he who prided himself on his fair government and his justice, who had sought to remedy the excesses of the Kakizuki and had expected Heaven to smile on him.

After the water receded a little, and the mud and debris had been cleared from the streets, Takaakira was ordered to go to the Prince Abbot at Ryusonji to find out what had gone wrong.

Trees had fallen in the garden of the temple and stone lanterns lay smashed. The lake was muddy, brimming over, logs, branches, and leaves swirling in a whirlpool around its center. It was still raining and the sound of water was everywhere, not the usual pleasant trickling, but thunderous and threatening.

He was shown into the reception hall by a young monk with a badly scarred face. Takaakira was surprised someone so damaged served the Prince Abbot. He wondered if that, in itself, might be an insult to the gods. One could never be too careful.

A mournful singing echoed in the courtyard; he looked toward the sound and saw an old blind man, with a lute, sitting cross-legged on the veranda. The words of the song were inaudible in the rain. Something felt wrong to him. The back of his neck prickled. He had come to Ryusonji hoping to discover the cause of all their problems. Now he began to suspect that Ryusonji itself was the cause.

It was the first time he had met the Prince Abbot face-to-face, though he had seen him at a distance at the ceremonies to give thanks for the Miboshi victory and install the new emperor. Then and now, the priest had an impressive authority. If he was disturbed by recent events he gave no sign of it. He seemed completely in control of himself and of all he commanded, seen and unseen.

Yet water dripped through the roof, puddling on the wooden floors, staining the matting, punctuating their tense exchange.

The young monk with the scarred face knelt on one side of the Prince Abbot. On the other was an older man, strong and serious-looking, who was making notes of their conversation with a small badger-hair brush. After formalities had been traded, Takaakira sat in silence for a few moments, wondering how best to broach his concerns, which he realized were more complicated than he had at first thought. The Prince Abbot had been responsible for the success of the Miboshi, the death of the Crown Prince, and the accession of the new emperor. It went without saying that Lord Aritomo needed his support in the spiritual realm, as the priest needed his in the physical. Despite the Prince Abbot's calm air, Takaakira sensed an imbalance here in the heart of the realm. He thought, *A man is at his most dangerous when he senses his powers beginning to slip from him.*

Finally the Prince Abbot spoke. "The former prince's son, Yoshimori, escaped from the palace with his nurse's daughter, the so-called Autumn Princess."

"He is still alive?" Takaakira felt the shock of this revelation deep in his gut.

"He was a few months ago. In the fourth month the man I sent caught up with them. But he has not returned with the child's head as he was ordered to."

"Do you know where Yoshimori is now?"

"Presumably somewhere in the Darkwood, if he has survived."

"You should have informed us earlier," Takaakira said sternly. "Lord Aritomo would raze the Darkwood if it meant he would find Yoshimori there. What sort of man did you send? A monk? A warrior?"

"A young acolyte of mine. It's possible I made a mistake . . . I cannot reveal too much to you as these are esoteric matters. I can tell you that he is known as Shikanoko. He is the nephew of Kumayama no Jiro no Sademasa. He has an affinity with the forest, which is why I believe he will be found in the Darkwood."

Sademasa, who had been a vassal of Kiyoyori's, had sworn allegiance to the Miboshi during their advance on the capital. Takaakira stored that information away without comment, and said, "I am an initiate. You may speak of these things to me."

The Prince Abbot gave him a quick sharp glance, as though seeing him with new eyes and needing to reassess his opinion.

"Very well. I believed Shikanoko was destined by Heaven to be a powerful sage, for fate led him not only to me but to two or three other people of great ability and deep knowledge of the other worlds: a mountain sorcerer, a woman of whom I know very little, and the old man you might have seen on your way in."

"The lute player?" Takaakira said, in surprise.

"Yes, once my equal in all spiritual matters. He had been living in Kiyoyori's household for years, unknown to anyone until I discovered him. I sent Gessho to bring him to me." He indicated the older monk, who stopped writing for a moment and bowed his head in response.

"Gessho found him with Shikanoko. In fact they had fallen into the hands of Sademasa, which would be neither here nor there if Sademasa had not subsequently decided to abandon the Kakizuki and ally himself with the Miboshi. He is still waiting for his reward from me."

"When the old man arrived here," Gessho said, "he was as he is now, practically senile."

"Was he always blind?" Takaakira asked.

"Kiyoyori's wife put out his eyes," Gessho said. "I saw them fixed to the gate at Matsutani."

"Did they still see?" Takaakira tried to keep his voice emotionless, but the cruelty, and the casual way Gessho spoke of it, shocked him.

"Yes, they saw everything," Gessho said quietly. "We said prayers over them and I hope we placated them. But Matsutani was badly damaged by the earthquake. Who knows if the eyes are still there?"

"Well, Sesshin and his eyes are not my main concern at the moment," the Prince Abbot said. "Shikanoko is, and, even more, Yoshimori. If he falls into the hands of the Kakizuki he will become an inspiration to them, a rallying point."

He is the true emperor, Takaakira realized. *No wonder the realm is so afflicted by disaster and suffering.* And then he thought with dread, *What have we done?*

There was no turning back now. He put the fear from him and said, "It is a most unfortunate state of affairs. I hesitate to report it to Lord Aritomo, yet he must be told. But I need some strategy to soften the blow. Do you have any suggestions?"

"Let me send someone into the Darkwood. Gessho tracked Shikanoko once; he can do it again."

"I will go gladly," Gessho exclaimed, his voice sounding suddenly loud, for they had all been almost whispering.

"My lord Abbot!" The young monk with the scarred face spoke for the first time. "Send me with Gessho. I have my disfigurement and weeks of pain for which to claim payment."

"I am to blame for that." The priest took him by the

hand and drew him close. "Leave your revenge to me and be assured he will pay tenfold."

Takaakira sat in thought for a few moments. To launch a major manhunt for the fugitives would signal clearly that Yoshimori was alive and rekindle all the Kakizuki hopes. It might be better to follow the Prince Abbot's advice, at least in the first instance.

"Do nothing until I have spoken to his lordship," he said, and abruptly took his leave.

As he passed through the courtyard he heard the blind man's voice again. This time he could make out the words.

The dragon child, he flew too high
He was still so young, he tried his best.
But his wings failed and he fell to earth . . .

Takaakira decided the old man needed to be questioned a little more forcefully.

"Yoshimori escaped?" Lord Aritomo had been glancing impatiently around the room in the former Kakizuki palace, but now he turned his fierce gaze on Takaakira. "Who rescued him? I'll burn them alive!"

"The girl they call the Autumn Princess, apparently," Takaakira replied.

"Ah, Hidetake's daughter. Only child, sixteen years old. Her mother was Yoshimori's nurse."

Takaakira was not surprised his lord knew this. He had

a phenomenal memory for details of lineage and relationships, the complex interlocking of noble families. "And a young man called Shikanoko was involved, an acolyte of the Prince Abbot's, also the nephew of the Kumayama lord."

"Sademasa? He's an ally of ours now. Shikanoko is a strange name. Why would he be called that?"

"I can't tell you," Takaakira replied. "All I know is, he is on his way to becoming a sorcerer."

"Is it his sorcery at work? Does that explain all these disasters, I wonder?" Aritomo mused to himself, looking away from Takaakira to the garden. Another typhoon was imminent, the sky almost as dark as night, a warm wind moaning over the curved roof and sighing in the eaves. Loose shutters were banging and a dog was howling. "Surely the typhoon season should be over?"

Aritomo was of small, slight stature. Had Takaakira been standing he would have towered over him, but he would rather face ten men at once, as he had at Shimaura, than bring bad news like this to his lord. Aritomo had already mentioned fire, which was an ominous sign. He liked to watch people burn. His punishments were as severe as his pride in his justice.

"Have we offended Heaven?" he dared to suggest, but Aritomo cut him off.

"We are carrying out the will of Heaven!" he shouted. He did not often raise his voice, but when he did it was terrifying. "If Heaven is displeased it is because we did not exterminate the whole nest of vipers but let the young escape! So, where is this snakeling?"

"His Eminence, the Prince Abbot, is of the opinion Shikanoko fled into the Darkwood and took Yoshimori with him."

"I will cut it down and burn him out!"

Takaakira had said the same thing to the Prince Abbot, but the truth was this was beyond even Aritomo's great power. The Darkwood stretched as far as the wild northern coast, over the spine of the country with its huge snow-covered mountains. He did not think it wise to mention this, but instead said tentatively, "There is a monk who wants to pursue them—"

"A monk? What good is a monk? Better to send a hundred warriors."

"This monk is a warrior, and he can be sent without drawing attention to Yoshimori's existence."

Aritomo clicked his teeth and shifted his jaw from side to side, a habit of his when he was thinking. "Who thinks they can survive the winter with a seven-year-old boy in the Darkwood? Hidetake had an estate on Lake Kasumi; Nishimi it is called. It is quite remote, but easily reached from the west, from Rakuhara. If I were trying to get the young Emperor—not that he is the Emperor, let that be understood—to his Kakizuki supporters I would try to take him there, to my father's old home."

"That is a brilliant deduction, lord," Takaakira said.

"I am trying to think like a girl," Aritomo replied. "It is not hard. Where else would she go? I suppose she would try Rinrakuji . . . yes . . . her father would have told her to go there, but, finding it burning, she would turn to the west." He gave a slight, tight-lipped smile. "I always try to see through the other person's eyes. Once you understand your enemy, you have defeated him. The Prince Abbot is a powerful force. I do not wish to offend him, but nor do I wish to fight his battles for him. Let his monk go after the sorcerer. You may go to Nishimi. Take a few men, not too many. We don't want to frighten our princess away. I guarantee she will turn up there before winter, with her young charge."

"You are sending me away from the capital?" Takaakira tried to sound reluctant, tried to hide that his mind was racing with plans for Hina.

"Your work here is mostly completed, isn't it?" Aritomo said. "This mission, anyway, is far more important."

"I will leave as soon as the storm is over," Takaakira said.

He touched his head to the ground and began to shuffle out backward. As the door slid open behind him, Aritomo said, "By the way, the fellow you recruited as a spy, Kiyoyori's brother."

"Masachika," Takaakira said unnecessarily.

"Make sure he is not changing sides again. Is he doing anything useful? If not, you can get rid of him. No one's going to miss him."

Maybe I should, Takaakira thought. *If he brings nothing useful back from Rakuhara, I will.*

The wind had risen to a shriek and the rain grew heavier as he went home. The ox baulked and the wheels of the carriage stuck in the mud. He got out and walked to the house, arriving soaked. Rain poured from the eaves. Behind its curtain, Hina waited on the veranda.

"I was worried about you," she cried artlessly.

"Yes, another typhoon is coming. I got back just in time. We will be shut indoors for a few days. After that we are going away."

He led her inside, as the servants ran to close the shutters and light lamps. He changed into dry clothes, noting with faint distaste how the room already smelled of mildew.

Hina knelt on the floor to pour wine for him. He thought she looked more mature, her face rounder, her figure slightly more curved. He longed for her to be old enough. Impatience coursed through him, made worse by the incessant wind.

"Come and sit by me. I have a headache."

She moved closer. "I will stroke it away," she said.

He lay with his head on her lap while her small fingers ran over his temples and scalp. After a few moments she began to sing softly.

The dragon child flew too high,
He was still so young

"Where did you hear that song?" he asked, his eyes closed.

"I don't know. I like it, it's sad."

"I heard an old blind man sing it today. Sesshin." Did her fingers alter their gentle rhythm? "Did you know him?"

He had never spoken to her about her life before and she did not talk about it, either to him or, as far as he knew, to anyone else. They both acted as though she had fallen from the moon and had no past and no earthly ties.

"I don't remember," she said, dreamily.

Did she really not remember? Had shock and grief wiped out her former life? Or was she dissembling, in which case she was even cleverer than he thought?

Neither of them spoke for a few moments. Then Hina said, "Where are we going?"

"To a place on the lake, quite far away." *I must start making plans*, he thought. *How will I transport her there? I can hardly take her openly.*

He remembered Lord Aritomo's face when he talked of burning and tried not to think of the risks he was taking.

By the time the storm was over, Takaakira had decided Hina should travel in a palanquin, with Bara, the woman who looked after her. Bara was not the sort of person whom Takaakira would usually have employed, but most of the servants in the capital, men and women, had fled with their Kakizuki masters, and many of the rest had died in the fighting, the fires, or the famine during the summer. There was an annoying dearth of working people, maids, cooks, gardeners, and grooms. Hina seemed to like Bara, and when Takaakira bothered to notice her, which was not often, he thought she was intelligent and kind.

There were two rather elegant elderly women who instructed Hina in various arts and skills, but he did not want his traveling group to be too large, so he made arrangements for them to follow by boat across the lake from Kasumiguchi when the weather allowed.

The palanquin waited at the stone step; the horses stood ready at the gate. It was daybreak and, throughout the city, roosters were crowing and birds singing in the gardens. After the storm, the air was fresh, almost chill, with the first hint of winter. Bara was on the veranda, but there was no sign of Hina.

"Where is the young lady?" he asked.

"She ran back to fetch something. She did not want to tell me what it was," Bara replied. "She gave me this." She showed Takaakira the Kudzu Vine Treasure Store.

He nodded. "I suppose she would not go without that. I will go and find her."

As he went inside he saw Hina walking toward him. She was wearing traveling clothes and holding the same box that had been in her hands when he had first discovered her, in the deserted house. He had not seen it since then and had put it out of his mind. Now he realized she had kept it hidden from him for months. He thought he knew everything about her, controlled every aspect of her life, but here was something secret.

"You don't have to bring that with you. Leave it here. It will be quite safe. Most of the servants are staying in the house."

She clutched the box more tightly and said, "I have to bring it."

"Show me what is inside," he said, eager to get away. "I will decide."

She said as she had before, "No."

"I am like a father to you and, one day, I will be your husband. I expect you to obey me. Let me see what is in the box, what is so important to you."

She sighed in the same adult way as when he first met her and his heart twisted with love for her. He wanted to say it did not matter, she could take whatever she liked, but now he had insisted, he could not back down.

She opened the box. The eyes lay there perfectly preserved, the dark irises, the black pupils, the whites glistening, viscous. They gazed at him unblinking, as if they saw everything he was and would ever be, and suddenly he could see only that, too. He saw his outward appearance, his own body beneath the green hunting robe, his long limbs, his angular features, his dark hair and eyes. He struggled to find his own vision again, to see Hina, the room, anything.

The eyes peered deeper, into mind, memory, and soul. He saw the men he had tortured and killed, the intrigues and betrayals that had brought him to Lord Aritomo's side, the women abandoned, his wife in far-off Yukikuni, the Snow Country.

"Close the lid," he whispered to Hina.

Of course, he should take the box at once to Ryusonji, to the Prince Abbot. For the eyes must be Sesshin's, plucked out at Matsutani, and now able to work some powerful magic. But then he would have to explain how he had come by them, and Hina would be discovered. His only desire, at that moment, was to get her away from the city to where she would be safe.

"Don't ever show them to anyone," he said, and hurried her into the palanquin.

5

SHIKANOKO

The monk Gessho left the capital around the same time, early in the tenth month. He traveled alone, apart from a werehawk the Prince Abbot had entrusted to him. He did not need anyone else; he had complete confidence in his physical and spiritual powers and a certain contempt for Shikanoko, despising his animal affiliation, knowing he had never experienced the extreme discipline of body and mind through which older monks, like himself, became initiates.

The lord, Aritomo's favorite, who visited the Prince Abbot had claimed to be an initiate. Gessho had been laughing inwardly, so much that he had made a rare mistake in his writing. Now the memory made him smile again. Noblemen and warriors dabbled in the mysteries, but the distractions of their lives, in particular their attachment to their women and children, prevented them from achieving true knowledge. No human ties held him down, and he knew his master, whom he admired more than anyone in the world, was the same. The Prince Abbot might seem to have great affection for his acolytes and his monks, but he would sacrifice them without hesitation in his pursuit of authority and knowledge.

Gessho's orders were clear. All three fugitives were to be killed. Yoshimori's head was to be brought back to the capital. The other two, the deer's child and the Autumn Princess, could be left to rot in the forest. *Let the animals he loves so much feed on him*, Gessho thought.

He did not think it would be hard to track them down. He was armed, with sword, knife, bow and arrows. He had been provided with a fine horse—he was equally at ease on horseback or in prayer; riding put him in a state, both relaxed and alert, that he found to be quite meditative. He knew the Darkwood well, having lived in it for more than ten years as a mountain hermit. The last the Prince Abbot had known of Shikanoko had been on the road to Rinrakuji, when one of the werehawks had apparently died, spending its last heartbeat to reach its master's mind and say farewell, and then outside a mountain hut, where he had seen the stag manifestation.

Gessho thought he could place the hut, recalling Akuzenji, who had ruled the mountain in the days when he had lived there. He decided to go toward Rinrakuji, taking the coast road to Shimaura and then turning north. However, his route took him directly past Matsutani and on the spur of the moment he decided to call in there. Shikanoko had

lived there for several months, the estate had been a Kakizuki stronghold under Kiyoyori, there were probably servants
left who would be loyal to their fallen lord and sympathetic
to his lost cause. There was a slight chance those he pursued might have taken refuge there.

He arrived at the residence just before dusk. He had
heard it had been badly damaged by an earthquake at the
beginning of the year. There were signs of new stonework
around the lake, and repairs had started on the gate where
he had seen Sesshin's eyes, but the eyes were no longer there,
the house still stood half-burned, the former stables a pile
of charred wood, while unused lumber lay on the ground,
half-buried by rank autumn grass.

He thought the house was deserted, but he could sense
the spiritual realm in a way others could not and slowly
became convinced that there was *something* inhabiting the
house. He wondered if it had been possessed by supernatural beings. He did not want to risk an encounter with them
that would delay his mission, and had decided to ride on,
a little disappointed as he had hoped to find shelter for
the night, when he saw a man approaching, carrying a
flask of wine, sprigs of bush clover, and a pot filled with
honeycomb.

He greeted the monk, making an awkward bow and
saying, "Welcome! I saw you coming and wanted to prevent you entering. The house has been taken over by spirits.
They allow me to go in with gifts for them, but anyone
else is attacked. They are quite malicious, there have been
several deaths."

Gessho frowned. "What sort of spirits are they?"

"From what I've been told I believe they are guardians, put in place by Master Sesshin when he lived here. Since his unfortunate downfall, they have become spiteful. Only he can control them, I fear, but will he ever return?"

"I am Gessho from Ryusonji," the monk said. "Sesshin is there now. He has become a lute player. My master with great kindness took him in and had him taught music. But even if he were here he would be no use. His powers are gone."

"Lady Tama is growing desperate," the man said, with unpleasant familiarity. "The estate was granted to her, it has been her home all her life, but she cannot repair the house or live in it. Yet if she abandons it, she has nowhere else to go and no other choice but to become a nun."

Which no doubt would not suit you, Gessho thought.

"I am just a retainer," the other hastened to say, as though reading his mind. "Hisoku is my name. I am completely at your service and would appreciate your favor." He paused and then said, "Well, I must make these offerings before the spirits grow impatient. But come with me afterward to the house where we are staying. We would be very grateful for any advice a wise monk like yourself could give us. You must stop for the night before you ride on. Where are you going? Few people ride toward the Darkwood these days."

"I will tell you later." Gessho watched Hisoku approach the veranda of the ruined house. He had to step carefully among an array of household objects, brooms, cushions, pots, ladles, scoops, which had all obviously been flung out of the house. They had been crafted with care, they were once precious and useful, but for weeks they had lain neglected under sun and wind and now had something forlorn, almost repulsive about them. Gessho felt a shiver of disgust touch his spine. All that mess should be cleared away for a start, though he himself was reluctant to touch anything.

Hisoku went cautiously forward, stepped onto the veranda, and placed his gifts just inside the open door. He struck a bronze bowl, which rang out in a clear, piercing note, and bowed deeply.

Gessho heard indistinct voices, making another shiver pass through his spine. His horse put its ears back and tried to spin away. While he was controlling it, Hisoku came back looking anxious.

"They asked who you were and, when I told them, they said you should go back to Ryusonji, at once."

"I will deal with them," Gessho said. "In the morning, I will get rid of them."

A shadow passed over their heads and the werehawk settled on the gatepost. It gave a shriek, and from the house came an answering yell. A small writing desk and an inkstone were hurled out, landing with a crash in the garden.

"Oh, don't make them angry," Hisoku cried. "It will only make things worse."

"You have spoiled them and indulged them," Gessho said, making little effort to hide his contempt. "Spirits have to be treated with a firm hand and shown who is master."

"At least they let me go into the house from time to time, and so far have not killed me. Many others have died."

Gessho thought the situation was intolerable, and he told Lady Tama so, after she and Haru, in whose house they were staying, had served dinner. The food was surprisingly good, river fish with grilled yams, quails' eggs, and bean curd.

"Your estate is obviously rich—you cannot let these errant spirits destroy it."

"You must have been sent by Heaven," she replied. "Surely a monk of your learning and holiness can exorcise them. I am afraid it is my fault for treating Master Sesshin so badly, but I am filled with remorse now and ready to make whatever amends I can."

"I will do my best to remove them, but I cannot stay long. I have my own mission."

He asked if they had seen or heard of Shikanoko in the past few months.

"Who is that?" Hisoku replied.

"He was the Prince Abbot's acolyte," Gessho explained briefly, "but he did not return from a journey he was sent on in the fourth month. We fear he died and His Holiness wishes to retrieve his body, due to his great affection for him."

"I have not seen him," Tama said. "Poor young man, I treated him badly, too."

Gessho wondered how genuine her remorse was. He discerned her character to be deep and possibly duplicitous.

"I will now spend some time in meditation," he announced. "I will speak to the spirits tomorrow, before I leave."

He took fresh flowers and rice gruel from the morning meal. As he approached the house, he heard the spirits talking to each other.

"Oh, here he comes, the fine monk from the capital."

"He thinks he will make us do what he wants."

"We don't do what anyone wants, do we?"

"We only do what *we* want."

Gessho laid the offerings down on the veranda and knelt in silence, his eyes closed, summoning up all his spiritual strength, calling on the name of the Enlightened One.

"Oh, he's a mighty monk!"

"He is mighty! Are you frightened?"

"No, I'm not frightened yet. Are you?"

"Not yet. But I might be soon."

They both began to cackle with laughter.

"I command you to leave this place," Gessho said in a booming voice.

"Ha-ha, he's wonderful, isn't he?"

"He's so wonderful, I think we should leave."

"But we're not going to."

"We should do something for him, though."

"We could tell him what happens to him when he goes into the Darkwood."

"What, that he loses his head? No, that's too sad. Tell him something nice. Tell him about the eyes."

"Oh, yes, the eyes are nice. Gessho!"

"I am listening," the monk replied.

"We can leave only if our master's eyes are replaced. Then we will go back to the gateposts where he first established us. There, that's fair, isn't it?"

"I don't really want to go back. I like it here."

"I like it here, too. It's much better than the gateposts. But don't worry, the eyes are lost. No one's ever going to find them. We can stay here forever."

"They are not lost," the second spirit said sulkily. "Kiyoyori's daughter took them."

"She's dead, isn't she? Kiyoyori's daughter, isn't she dead?"

"Maybe she is and maybe she isn't."

There was the sound of a smack and a yell of pain.

Gessho said, "So, if your master's eyes are found, you will leave the house and return to the gateposts?"

"Yes, we will have to."

"But if you go into the Darkwood, you will not live to see it." They both shrieked with laughter again.

Gessho next tried flattery, thanking them for their warning and praising them for their insight, but though that seemed to please them insofar as they did not throw anything at his head, he could not persuade them to move.

He returned to Haru's house, eager to ride on into the Darkwood. The spirits' warnings had not dissuaded him but rather the opposite. If he risked losing his head it could only mean someone of great skill and power was waiting for him. He relished the idea of the encounter.

"What happened to the daughter?" he asked Haru, finding her alone in the kitchen.

"Lady Hina?" Haru said. "We believe she is dead. My

lady has been grieving for her as well as for her son, and her husband. You will have noticed how low her spirits are."

"Could Hina have perhaps survived?"

"How would we ever know unless she found her way back here?"

"It will be more difficult to remove the spirits than I thought. The house will have to be abandoned. I suppose Shikanoko might be able to control them."

"But you believe Shikanoko to be dead, don't you?"

Her eyes were fixed on his face and he regretted saying so much.

"The Prince Abbot must be a warmhearted man to send a great monk like you in search of a pile of bones!" she said.

Gessho made no direct response but remarked after a few moments, seemingly idly, "There are no men around apart from Hisoku. Where are they all? Where is your husband?"

"Most died at Shimaura. Their heads were displayed there all summer. The rest perished in the capital alongside Lord Kiyoyori."

"Your husband among them?"

She nodded her head, looking away, like a woman not comfortable with lying, then busied herself with preparing food for him to take on the journey.

Gessho watched her all the time and made her eat one of the rice balls before tucking the rest away in his pouch. As he rode away he glanced back over his shoulder and saw her talking to a boy aged about ten, her son presumably. All morning, as he followed the stream to the northeast, he was aware the boy was following him. He wondered if it was just some childish game—he remembered doing the same thing as a boy—or if Haru had sent him with some other purpose in mind. He did not trust her, nor did he believe her husband was dead.

The path forked and Gessho went a little way up the left-hand branch and guided the horse into the bushes. The boy appeared and took the right-hand branch without hesitation. Gessho waited a short while and then dismounted, tied the horse to a tree, and, silent and unseen, followed the boy.

The path looked tangled and overgrown, but he could see that brushwood had been cut and dragged over it. Beneath the branches were signs it was well trodden. He did not want to go too far from his horse, but just as he was about to turn back the undergrowth cleared and he found himself on top of a steep crag. Below was a small wooden fortress. On its roof flew the red banners of the Kakizuki and the three black cedars of Kuromori.

There was no sign of the boy. Either he had moved faster than Gessho thought or there was some secret path he had taken, maybe a tunnel he had slipped through, to get to the fortress.

Smoke rose from cooking fires and men's voices carried across the ravine. The morning sun glinted on spearheads. It outraged him to see this Kakizuki stronghold in what should have been Miboshi-held land as far as Minatogura. So the last of Kiyoyori's men were holding out here, that lying woman's husband, no doubt, among them.

He slipped back into the undergrowth and for a few

moments considered what he might do next. He wondered what message the boy had taken to his father and if it had any bearing on him. He did not think the men would leave the safety of their stronghold to pursue a solitary monk. All the same, their defiance would have to be dealt with. The next estate to the east was Kumayama, where he had caught up with Shikanoko before. He decided he would make his way there in a few days, if he had not had any success in his early search. He would replenish his food supplies, and suggest to Sademasa, the uncle who had switched sides, that it would be in his interests to deal with the men at Kuromori.

He returned swiftly to where he had left the horse and continued up the left-hand path, riding for the rest of the day. At nightfall he dismounted and let the horse drink from the stream and graze while he slept for a few hours, drifting in and out of dreams in which he was a boy again. He saw his mother's form in the distance and ran to catch up with her, but fell down through the earth, waking with a start. He rose shortly after midnight, as had been his custom for years, washed his face in the cold stream water, and sat in meditation, listening to the sounds of the nighttime forest. Once a wolf howled far in the distance, and he heard the feathery sigh of an owl's wings as it returned to roost. He saw it blink its yellow eyes at the horse, which stood dozing, one hind leg locked in, beneath the owl's tree. The werehawk slept, perched on the horse's back. Overhead, the stars shone in a clear sky across which, from time to time, drifted swathes of haze. While it was still dark, the first birds began to pipe up, pigeons, doves, robins, and, as day broke, thrushes. It was not the exuberant chorus of spring but autumn's more melancholy song, breeding and nesting over, winter's cold ahead.

He recognized the track he had followed in his earlier pursuit of Shikanoko, but in his meditation he had become aware of a strange presence, some dark magic at work, so instead of turning southward to Kumayama he decided to follow it, to the north at first, and then, when the mountains rose as an impassable barrier, to the east. The horse grew more nervous, laid its ears flat against its head, and shied frequently, once at the skeleton of a stag lying at the foot of a huge cliff. Gessho stopped and dismounted to see if its antlers remained, for they had many uses in medicine and ritual, but the skull and the antlers were gone. However, the shoulder blades remained and he took them with him. After that he noticed more piles of bones, stripped of all flesh, mostly bleached white but some green with age. The horse trembled and jigged past them. The werehawk flew down and inspected them, its golden eyes glinting. They seemed to be mostly animal, but two or three were human, though no trace of clothing, armor, or weapons could be seen. Foxes and crows might have picked their bones, but a person, or people, must have pilfered everything else, unless it was the tengu who were said to dwell in the Darkwood.

On the fourth day the smell began, at first a faint whiff that from time to time hit his nostrils, then, as he felt he was growing closer to the source of the magic, an odor so strong it blotted out everything else. Gessho urged the horse forward and it obeyed reluctantly; they were both alert to every sound.

Gessho heard the wolves before he saw them, a snarling rush, a pad of feet. The werehawk screamed. The horse spun and bucked in terror, then reared upright, so high Gessho thought it was going to fall backward. He leaped from its back, drawing his sword in the same moment. The horse lashed out with its rear legs and hit one of the wolves in the flank, hurling it a few paces away, where it lay whimpering. Gessho thrust his sword into the chest of the second as it came at him, teeth bared. The horse galloped off, crashing through the undergrowth. The third wolf backed off, snarling, then turned and ran away in the opposite direction.

Gessho pulled the bow from his back and set an arrow to it. The forest grew so thickly it was hard to shoot properly. The first arrow hit the trunk of a tree; the second skimmed over the wolf's back, making it somersault, but it found its feet rapidly and ran on. Gessho ran after it, branches lashing and clawing at him. The first wolf recovered from the horse's kick and pursued him, limping but swift, made fiercer by pain.

The smell grew fouler, making him double up and gag. He crossed a stream, jumping from stone to stone. The wolf caught up with him on the farther bank. It tried to attack him, but its injuries hampered it, making it easy enough to dispatch with his knife. He drove it deep into the animal's throat and let the body fall into the stream.

He stood on the bank, trying to catch his breath, wondering if he was dreaming, for, though he had traveled all over the Eight Islands and had taken part in countless extreme secret rituals, he had never in his life seen anything like the scene before him.

Rocks like animals turned to stone; carved statues with lacquered skulls; animals that had once lived and were preserved, still lifelike; creatures that had never been conceived within a mother or borne by her, but that had a sort of life and that moved and walked and watched his approach with their blue gem eyes; birds that flapped the carefully woven and glued feathers of their wings and turned their empty skulls toward him.

He transferred the knife to his left hand and drew his sword with his right, raising it threateningly if any animal came too close. They made his skin crawl in disgust. He understood the pollution and profanity to which he was exposing himself and feared he would never be clean again. Even when he had lived in the Darkwood himself, he had never imagined such a place might exist within it. *The whole thing must be cleared*, he thought. *We will scour it from end to end and rid it of this vile old magic.*

Muttering incantations, the hidden names of the Enlightened One, the secret words known only to initiates, he went forward into the clearing, to a hut with walls of animal skins and a roof of bones. There was no way of approaching silently. The horde of animals and birds was already uttering cries and howls of alarm, which rang through the clearing and echoed back from the surrounding mountains.

Gessho, characteristically, turned this to his advantage, shouting at the top of his voice, "I am Gessho of Ryusonji. By the authority of the Prince Abbot, I command whoever is the source and cause of this abhorrence to reveal himself."

He saw a movement on the slope behind the hut. Someone was hastening down, taking great leaps over logs and boulders. Gessho sheathed his sword and quickly put an arrow to his bow, muttering a binding spell to it. Even as he loosed it he felt an opposing magic and knew it would go wide.

He took another and shot swiftly. A crow-like bird with an eagle's head dived onto the arrow in mid-flight, grasped it in its beak, and flew away with it. The werehawk pursued it, shrieking in rage.

Gessho flung the bow down and drew his sword again. He sensed someone behind him and turned, slashing wildly, but there was no one there, or no one visible, for he was sure he caught a shadow of movement.

Then the throb of magic in the air grew stronger, making him spin back. Someone—it had to be the sorcerer—was standing at the edge of the clearing, a few hundred paces away.

Gessho called, "I command you, in the name of the Emperor, and his uncle, the Prince Abbot of Ryusonji, to submit to me and surrender any fugitives you are hiding."

"There are no fugitives here," the man replied. "Only those who belong to the forest. You are the stranger, the intruder. Or maybe you are the fugitive, escaping from an unjust, cruel master. In which case, lay down your weapons and be welcome."

"There is worse perversion here than I have ever seen in my life," Gessho shouted in response.

"Then you do not know your master's heart," the sorcerer called back, in a voice of extraordinary clarity.

Enraged, the monk rushed forward, sword raised. In his path the air seemed to shimmer and suddenly a young boy stood before him, a handsome lad with a calm face and an ethereal smile. Gessho halted, his reason telling him it must be an imp of some sort, or an illusion created by the sorcerer, his mind wondering if it could be Yoshimori himself, his heart pierced suddenly by the fragile, innocent beauty before him.

In wonder, he leaned forward to look at him and the boy smiled more widely, opening his mouth, showing small white teeth. From behind those teeth came a stream of tiny darts, spat into Gessho's eyes.

He knew at once that they were poisoned, for they burned agonizingly, like a bee's sting. As he gritted his teeth against the pain, he felt an invisible being leap onto his back and slip something around his neck, a leather strap that he struggled in vain to break. He arched his back and flexed his huge shoulders and felt the leather give slightly. He thrust his fingers under it and wrenched it away. As he flung it down, the creature holding it came shimmering into view. It was another boy, the same age as the first and strikingly similar, although his features were distorted by an animal-like snarl.

Shadows darkened Gessho's vision, but his enormous strength was not yet exhausted and he still held his sword. It was protected by powerful prayers and would not be subject to the sorcerer's magic. He struck out at the second boy, only to see him leap into the air, like a monkey, out of his range. Then he realized imps surrounded him on all sides. They were tormenting him like a swarm of hornets, disappearing and reappearing, darting in to stab his legs, or flying past him leaving wounds in his neck and face.

He was bleeding from a dozen cuts but was still far from giving up when he heard hoof beats and splashing and, turning, saw his horse cross the stream with Shikanoko on its back. The boys fell back, giving him a moment's respite.

"Shikanoko," Gessho called. "The Prince Abbot commands you to return to Ryusonji. Where is Yoshimori?"

"So this is your horse, Gessho," Shikanoko replied, leaping to the ground. "But why have you come on this doomed journey? Now I'll have to kill you."

"Come back with me and you won't have to kill me," Gessho said boldly.

Shika replied, "I would tell you to inform your master that I will return to Ryusonji for one purpose only, which will be to destroy him, but you will not see him again until he meets you in Hell."

Gessho called to the werehawk, circling overhead. "Fly, fly to Ryusonji. Tell my lord what became of me, and where."

Shikanoko snapped his fingers and the bird flew to his shoulder.

Gessho knew then that all was lost and his life was over. He heard the voices of the spirits in Matsutani.

We could tell him what happens to him when he goes into the Darkwood.

What, that he loses his head? No, that's too sad.

And it was too sad, that he should be undone by sorcery and magic, he who had never yet lost an argument or a fight. His eyes filled with water, tears mingling with his blood. He remembered his dream of his mother.

"Stand back," Shikanoko said to the boys. "We will fight with swords, now."

"Where is Yoshimori?" Gessho demanded, as they began to circle each other.

Shikanoko did not answer.

"Do you have him here? Tell me!"

The animals had fallen silent. Out of the corner of his eye Gessho saw the sorcerer approaching, his straggling hair, his gleaming eyes. He sensed his aura of magical power. He could fight a swordsman, he could strive against a magician, but he could not do both at the same time, and he feared the magic more than the sword. The animals, false and real, turned their heads toward their master, waiting for his command. It would take only one word from them and they would attack him. The idea of his death being delivered by their fake mouths, their wooden teeth, their metal claws, filled him with revulsion and desolation.

Shikanoko was becoming impatient, making ever fiercer thrusts and slashes, which Gessho parried, able with his greater strength to drive the younger man back. With each circle he moved closer to the watching sorcerer. When he judged the distance was right he leaped backward, as though avoiding Shikanoko's sword, and, turning in midair, his knife in his left hand, stabbed the sorcerer in the throat as he landed.

For a moment he regretted not taking the old man hostage and forcing Shikanoko to submit, but he did not think he and his troop of imps would be swayed by any human compassion. Gessho pulled out the knife, marveling that the sorcerer's blood spurted red and warm like any other man's, and then turned to face Shikanoko.

A howl of fear and desolation came from the animals, as their master and maker crumpled to the ground. Shikanoko, too, cried out in fury.

"The fight was between us! Well, now you will pay!"

His sword, Jinan, descended, slashing Gessho from shoulder to waist. Its returning stroke whipped through his neck, severing his head. The eyes stared for one final moment, blinked one last time. The body swayed and crashed like a felled cedar.

Shika stepped between the body and the head, ignoring the flowing blood, and knelt beside Shisoku, gripping his hands.

"You made me what I am," he said, tears falling down

his face. "You brought me back from the edge of death
despair."

The old man was beyond answering; he would ne
move or speak again, would no more create his stran
creatures nor practice his powerful haphazard magic. Tl
five boys gathered around.

Kiku said, "He asks you not to waste that fine skull."

"And to take care of the animals," Mu added.

Then they all wept bitterly for their teacher, one of their
five fathers, who, without knowing, taught them human
grief.

They gathered wood and made a pyre, watching as the
old sorcerer's corpse was reduced to ash. The animals
howled mournfully and even the insects gave out strange,
sad susurrations, all the melancholy sounds of autumn dis-
tilled like one of Shisoku's potions.

Shisoku burned like grass, but when they rolled Gessho's
body onto the pyre it smoked and sizzled like a roasting
boar, the smell mingling with the fragrant cedar branches.
Shika was going to burn the head, too, but Kiku took it
from him and buried it beneath a wooden marker.

The boys caught the werehawk in a net and killed it.
Kuro removed the beak, skin, feathers, and claws, and after
boiling the bones carefully so all the flesh came loose, buried the remains deep so the animals would not dig them up.
The boys ate many birds, but some instinct told them this
half-magic bird was poisonous. Kuro put the rest out to dry,
adding them to the bones on the roof, covering them with
the same net to keep the real birds away.

Shika was both sad and relieved the werehawk was dead. It could have been a useful spy, but on the other hand it might have switched allegiance at any moment and flown back to the Prince Abbot. He already knew that the birds were capricious and untrustworthy. He had the scars on his face to prove it. He mourned the death of Shisoku for many weeks, wishing he could have saved him, regretting that it was because of him that Gessho had found his way to the sorcerer's hut. The monk's appearance brought back memories of Ryusonji, of the Prince Abbot and his secret rituals. They made his skin crawl; he wondered if he would ever be free. At night he took out the mended mask, purified it with prayers and incense, and finally dared wear it again. Deep in the forest the stags bellowed, and from their calls he learned the movements of the autumn dance and its knowledge of resignation and death.

The boys grew and learned with supernatural ability. Kiku knew how to embalm and lacquer and could combine secret elements to make spirit-returning incense. Mu could forge steel and mend broken tools. Kuro was familiar with all the poisons of the forest, the plants, and the five deadly creatures, which he kept live, and tried to re-create when they died. Ima was good at tanning skins, and also knew all the forest plants and insects, though he was more interested in their healing properties and in the many remedies Shisoku had recorded in his own idiosyncratic code. He and Ku mostly looked after the animals, fed them

and patched them up. Morning and evening, all the boys repeated Shisoku's prayers and chants that protected the forest.

They played on the horse, a mature and good-natured creature that put up with them vaulting on its back and making it gallop around the clearing and jump over rocks and statues. They named it Kuri, for its coat was the same glossy shade as the chestnuts they collected in the forest.

Kiku, being the eldest, was usually the leader in all their activities and games, but he had a cruel streak that made the younger boys wary of him. Mu had a better sense of humor—Kiku never laughed from amusement or pure joy but only in mockery—and was kinder to the two youngest. There was a rivalry between the two older boys that led them to test each other and fight constantly. Shika had to forbid them to use actual weapons; instead, their tools of combat were the strange talents with which they had been born, the second self and invisibility, and these they practised endlessly. They were like fox or wolf cubs, perfecting, through play, all the skills they needed for adult life. They seemed to age a year every month, and not a day passed that Shika did not recall Sesshin's words, *They will be demons.* Sometimes he reflected he should have killed them the moment they were born, but now it was impossible. They had become precious to him. Their beauty and their strange skills intrigued and delighted him. He loved them as much as any man loves his sons, and he trained them as warriors' sons, for all the time he was planning strategies to take Kumayama.

About a month after the deaths of the sorcerer and the monk, when winter was setting in and the clouds filling up with snow, Shika was skinning a hare by the fire, watched hungrily by Gen, who had become enough of a wolf to eat real meat. He had just slit open the carcass and was scooping out the entrails when Kiku, also waiting by him, quivering like a dog at the smell of blood and raw flesh, said, "Someone is coming."

Shika could hear nothing besides the crackling of the fire and the panting of the animals, but he trusted Kiku's hearing, which grew more acute every day.

He skewered the hare and set it over the coals to roast. "Someone human? One or several?"

"One man on a horse."

Shika wiped the blood from his hands and stood. "Go to your positions," he said quietly. They had prepared for unwanted visitors. "Don't move unless I give you a signal."

Kuro held Kuri's muzzle to stop the horse neighing. Ima and Ku summoned the pack of dogs and wolves and hid with them behind the hut. Kiku and Mu picked up the bows Shika had made for them and took up position on either side of the ford across the stream, concealed behind rocks.

Shika waited in front of the hut, sword in hand.

A man rode across the stream on a dull-coated black horse, so thin Shika was surprised it could still move. Its hip bones stuck out, its back was swayed, its eyes sunken. He felt a pang of pity, for he recognized it as one of the famous Kuromori blacks, brother to Kiyoyori's own stallion. With that clue he identified the rider: Kiyoyori's retainer Kongyo, husband to Haru, the children's nurse.

Kongyo looked as half-starved as the horse. He slipped from its back and walked forward warily, his hand on his sword. His eyes glanced quickly around the clearing, taking in the skulls, the bone thatch, the clumps of feathers, the drying skins. He seemed to master a quiver of disgust and some other emotion when he smelled the roasting hare. The horse lowered its head and began to tear at the dying winter grass. Its belly gave a hollow rumble.

The two men stared at each other. Shika wondered if Kongyo knew him. It was more than a year since they had both served Lord Kiyoyori at Matsutani. Kongyo had been sent to Miyako before Lady Tama had put out Sesshin's eyes and turned him and Shika out into the Darkwood, but in the preceding weeks they had seen each other daily. Then, Kongyo had been the Kuromori lord's senior retainer and Shikanoko the dispossessed son of a dead warrior, tainted by his association with the bandit chief, Akuzenji. Now they stood on a more equal footing, determined by the fact that Kongyo was starving and Shika had food.

"Do you still call yourself Shikanoko?" Kongyo said finally.

Shika nodded briefly.

"I am Kuromori no Kongyo—"

"I know who you are," Shika interrupted. "How did you find your way here?"

"My son told me the monk Gessho had come back to find you. I sent him to follow Gessho; he marked the trail.

He saw Gessho die and he recognized you. You may remember him: he is the same age as Lady Hina and often played with her and her brother. We call him Chika."

"I remember him," Shika said, wondering how none of the boys had noticed him. They must have been too involved in the fight with Gessho, and then distracted by the death of Shisoku. And hadn't Chika prided himself on being able to flit around Matsutani unseen?

"He said you overcame Gessho partly by magic," Kongyo said, seeming to choose his words carefully as if anxious not to offend Shika. "That you employed spirits in the shape of children who could appear and disappear."

"Perhaps his shock at witnessing the death made him see delusions," Shika replied.

"But you have children here? We hoped one of them might be Yoshimori. Why else would the Prince Abbot send Gessho after you?" Kongyo's eyes were shining with a kind of mad hope. "If Yoshimori is alive, my lord did not die in vain."

Shika hesitated for a moment, but then decided he had nothing to fear from this starving man, who had been Kiyoyori's most loyal warrior. "Yoshimori is alive, but he is not here," he said. "I was with him, but I was injured, we were separated, and then, as your son saw, some other children came into my care and I could not leave them and go to look for him. Now it is nearly winter and soon it will snow. What can I do before spring?" He made a sign and one by one the boys appeared and gathered around them. Kongyo looked at them, taken aback by their appearance.

"They look as well suited to the forest as wolf cubs," he said finally. "But will a child of imperial blood, who has been raised in a palace, survive a winter in the Darkwood?"

"He is not alone," Shika replied, thinking with sorrow of Akihime, and the horses. "I can't explain everything to you now, but I believe he will be safe, until the time comes when he can be rescued and restored to the throne."

"We all pray that Heaven will decree it," Kongyo said solemnly. "But I have something else to tell you that I hope will encourage you to act. The night my son returned and told me he had seen you kill Gessho, I had a dream about you. I saw you as tall as a giant. Your head rested on the mountains of the north and your feet on the southern islands. I woke convinced Heaven has a plan for you. Why else should you have escaped death so many times? You were believed to have died when you fell off the mountain. Akuzenji could have killed you but he did not. My lord, Kiyoyori, spared you alone among the bandits. Your uncle captured you but handed you over to Gessho. The Prince Abbot did not put you to death but took you as his disciple. You escaped from his service, and now I find you here, alive, in this place of death."

"Maybe I have been lucky," Shika said. "You know a great deal about me."

"After the dream I pieced together all I had heard about you. And my wife told me she thought, along with everything else, that you had a kind heart, for you looked after Sesshin with tenderness after he was blinded. But it is not your luck, nor your kindness, important as they are, that will defeat the Prince Abbot. It is what you have learned from him, from Master Sesshin, and from the sorcerer who made these strange creatures."

"You are very flattering," Shika said, "but what exactly are you proposing?"

"We are confined to the fortress at Kuromori. We are starving—you can probably see that. We are not besieged as such. There is a secret passage through which individuals can slip in and out, but the roads all around are guarded and we believe Aritomo is planning another attack on the fortress. Masachika, Kiyoyori's brother, tried once before, but my son brought us a warning."

"He seems a useful lad."

"He is fearless and quite clever," Kongyo said with pride. "All Masachika's men were wiped out, but Masachika was spared. He agreed to switch sides, so we let him go—well, he is Kiyoyori's heir and Kakizuki by birth. None of us wanted his blood on our hands. We believe he went to the Kakizuki in Rakuhara, to tell them of our plight. We have heard nothing since then, but we feel Aritomo will launch an attack on Rakuhara in the spring. If you have taken your estate of Kumayama by then, you can relieve us at Kuromori and together we can surprise the Miboshi from the rear."

"And how will I take Kumayama with no men?"

"If Sademasa is dead his men will accept you for your father's sake. Matsutani is unoccupied, as it has been taken over by guardian spirits, but you will be able to deal with them. You will force a wedge between Miyako and Minatogura and cut off their supply lines."

"You have great confidence in me! How am I going to kill Sademasa?"

"With your imps and their magic, of course!" Kongyo gave him a sly glance. "Do you think that hare is cooked by now? You can think it over while we eat."

6

AKI

Akihime worried about her monthly bleeding, how she would manage in the forest, what she would tell Yoshi, if she should stay away from him—surely emperors had nothing to do with such polluting matter as menstrual blood—but the bleeding never came. She watched the monkeys mating, giving birth, nursing their young ones, the babies playing with the long pink nipples, and her own breasts ached and swelled. The old matriarch treated her like one of her many daughters, groomed her hair, which was growing out matted and wild, and gave her the pick of the seeds and fruits they collected as summer warmed the forest.

When it rained, the monkeys sat in the hot spring, and one damp day Aki took off her clothes and joined them. She could see that she had lost weight, her limbs no longer pleasingly plump, as they had been in the palace. Her collarbones protruded, but her stomach was very slightly rounded.

Yoshi had abandoned his clothes—once the rains began they were always wet—and he was turning as brown as a beechnut all over. His arms and legs were covered in cuts, scratches, and old scars. He never spoke of Kai—Aki wondered if he had forgotten her. He had joined the pack of young males and climbed and played with them all day long, coming to understand their chattering and facial gestures, sleeping in a heap with them at night. When they fled the palace Akihime had expected him not to be able to walk, but now he ran everywhere.

She tried to speak to him as much as possible, concerned he would forget human language. She sang to him and told him stories. The lute came alive under her fingers, enchanting the monkeys. He told her the names he had given to them. He called the matriarch Ame, the strongest male Hai, and his two special friends Shiro and Kemuri.

He rode the horses and persuaded Shiro and Kemuri to join him on their backs. To Aki's surprise, both horses put up with it. Yoshi never used saddle or bridle; he seemed to have developed a way of communicating with the horses as easily as with the monkeys, and both of them, even the bad-tempered Risu, did whatever he asked them, in a spirit of play.

The rains ended and the great heat of summer began. One day, the monkeys seemed unusually agitated. They gathered in groups, clutching one another, sniffing the air, peering to the northwest and chattering anxiously. Now and then, one of the young males, Shiro or Kemuri, bounded outward, calling threateningly, although Aki could not see or hear anything strange.

"What's wrong with them?" she asked Yoshi, who was sniffing the air, too.

"Someone is coming, someone they are afraid of."

Aki heard a pitiful crying, the noise the monkeys made when one of them died. It sent the group around her into even greater distress. A young female, in particular, began screaming in response. The distant crying became louder.

"It is one of them," Yoshi said. "One who was lost, a long time ago. I think he is tied up. He cannot come closer. He is calling for help."

"Don't go," Aki said. "It might be a trap."

"But he needs help."

"Someone might be using him as a decoy," she warned.

"What is a decoy?" Yoshi said, puzzled, but Aki did not have time to answer, for the whole monkey group, led by Ame and Hai, began to leap through the trees toward the sound. Kon hovered overhead, and Risu and Nyorin followed, with Aki walking between them. At first, the monkeys seemed cautious and furtive. They were drawn to the crying as if they could not help themselves, yet they were afraid. They wanted to keep silent, but the closer they came, the more their fear made them chatter and squeal. The monkey who was tied up cried even more loudly but now with a heartbreaking note of hope.

As they came to the edge of the clearing, Aki could see him clearly, a half-grown male, with a green collar round his neck, tethered to a post driven into the ground. The elders, Ame and Hai, made warning noises. Hai ran the length of the troop, cuffing the young males into submission, but Shiro and Kemuri dashed forward with Yoshi on their heels. Aki cried out to him, as he and the two monkeys ran into a net and were immediately trapped in its invisible, unbreakable mesh. The monkeys squealed in the same note as the captured one. Yoshi was shouting in rage.

The watching monkeys howled in horror, jumping in the air, thumping the ground with their fists. Aki was about to run forward, but Ame held out a hand to restrain her, tapping her own belly and then patting Aki's. Her bright, knowing eyes held Aki's for a moment. When the girl looked away she saw that three men had come into the clearing. They wore strange red clothes, and, even though two were fully grown, something about them, their hair maybe, was childlike. Aki recognized the third. It was the boy who had performed with the monkeys at Majima.

He went to the tied-up monkey and gave him some food as a reward, which the monkey crammed into his mouth, chortling gently as though pleased with himself. His previous distress had completely disappeared. When his owner untied him he jumped straightaway onto the boy's shoulder and began grooming his hair.

The other two men went to the net, shouting in surprise. "A good catch! Two young males and a boy!"

Again Aki wanted to run forward—but she was naked, and unarmed. She had left her knife and bow, along with Genzo, in the cave. The men carried knives and sticks. She remembered the men on the road to Rinrakuji. Shikanoko had appeared from nowhere and killed them, but if he had not, they would have raped her, and probably murdered or enslaved her. She was afraid these men would do the same. Then Yoshi would be lost completely. No one would know who he was and he would soon forget.

And she was stunned by something else: the realization that she was carrying a child.

She looked at the horses, who stood watching, ears pricked forward.

I will follow Risu, she thought. *Kiyoyori's spirit will tell me what to do.*

Risu did not move, nor did Nyorin. Yoshi did not look toward them, he did not utter another word, even when his captors questioned him. They were too amazed at their catch to notice anything else in the trees on the edge of the clearing.

"He must have been brought up by monkeys," the boy marveled. "Maybe he never learned to speak."

Aki remembered him at the market on the shore. He had seemed bold, kind to his monkey partners, and not slow to laugh at himself. Perhaps Yoshi would be safer away from her. He could disappear among the people of the riverbank. The Prince Abbot would never look for him there. He would be searching for a young noblewoman with a boy, and, of course, he or his monks would quickly recognize her. But none of them would have seen Yoshi since his first haircut ceremony, at eighteen months of age. He would be indistinguishable from all the other orphans and urchins struggling to survive. She would always know where to find him, with the monkey boy.

But watching him and his two friends being bound with ropes and led away made her heart break. Risu bent her neck and nuzzled Aki's shoulder. She took that to mean that Kiyoyori's spirit approved of her decision. She leaned against the mare's flanks.

"Hurry up and be born," she whispered. "I need you. You and my child will grow up as brothers."

From far above she heard a low fluting call and, looking up, she saw Kon, half-gold, half-black against the deep blue summer sky. The werehawk fluttered its wings as though to say farewell and flew off after the Emperor and his monkeys.

The lute lost its gold embossing and its mother-of-pearl inlay and went into a sulk. It refused to release its tunes, no matter how many times Aki took it out, polished it, cajoled it, even prayed to it. She wanted to be able to play it on her journey to give her a plausible reason for being on the road.

She knew she had to leave the Darkwood. She did not think she would survive a winter there, even with the hot springs, not with a baby, which she had calculated would be born in the first month. She did not want to give birth in the forest, alone. She needed other women around her to help her bring the child into the world. The only place she could think of to go was her old country home at Nishimi. Even though it was years since she had been there, surely the women, who had known her as a child, would look after her.

She began to make preparations, took the saddle from

where she had stowed it in the cave and wiped the mildew from it, washed her clothes in the spring, and tried to comb out her hair. It had grown enough to tie in bunches, like a country girl's. She bound the ends with strands of the tough reeds that grew in the shade around the pools.

The day she planned to leave, the monkeys' behavior puzzled her. They did not go out into the forest as they usually did from dawn but stayed close to the caves, chattering nervously. The horses, too, seemed restless, their coats dark with sweat.

By midday the air had turned metallic and the sky had darkened. The tops of the trees began to lash against one another, as a hot wind drove through them. Then rain fell, the drops sizzling as they hit the rocks and the ground. The surface of the pools churned. Soon the rain was so heavy it seemed to rise from the earth as much as it fell from the sky.

The whole world was made of water. Every tiny channel filled and overflowed. The wind howled more fiercely, driving the rain horizontally. There was a crack like thunder and the ground shook as a huge cedar was torn up by its roots and thrown down.

The monkeys huddled together, surrounding Aki and Ame, whimpering at every loud noise. Risu laid her ears back and stamped nervously. Nyorin stood motionless, gazing out at the curtains of rain.

When the typhoon had passed, they ventured outside. The earth steamed and a carpet of leaves and branches covered the ground. The monkeys investigated the fallen tree warily, finding grubs and insects in its roots. The storm had delivered a feast as well as destruction. Everything was washed clean and the air was sweet-smelling. One by one, the forest birds began to sing.

The young monkeys went out exploring, though they were still subdued and nervous after the capture of Shiro and Kemuri. Aki led the horses to find new grass. She could hear the monkeys chattering ahead of her and could follow the trail of twigs and seed casings they let fall from the trees. The horses grazed on the long, lush grass. Aki was hungry, too. She sucked on roots of grass and chewed unripe beech mast, but these made her stomach ache even more.

They were following some sort of path, made by foxes or deer, that led to a stream. There were tracks in the mud, paw prints and hooves. The monkeys' chattering grew louder and then she heard a cry of pain. Risu neighed in reply and rushed forward, barging past Aki, almost knocking her down.

On the far bank stood a young stag, its new antlers shining and hard. She held up the bow and twanged it. The stag raised its head and sniffed the air, then turned and bounded away. She realized she was trembling with fear. For a moment she had thought the stag would transform into Shikanoko. Had it been just an animal or was it a sign, a symbol perhaps of the child they had made together? She was suddenly certain it was. *I am carrying his son*, she thought with a mixture of sorrow and joy. And then she remembered her dream, the night she had fled the palace. She had seen the same stag in her dream.

The rocks at the stream's edge were covered in debris from the storm, washed down by the torrent of water, left there when the stream subsided. The monkeys had been sifting through it. Now there was red blood on the rocks and one of the monkeys was sucking its paw and crying. The others were jumping around something that gleamed on the rocks and making warning noises as if they had surprised a snake.

Risu gave a long groaning whinny, and for the first time Aki saw Risu's belly ripple as the unborn foal kicked and struggled within her. She went to the mare and tried to soothe her. The monkeys scattered at her approach and ran back to the treetops. Behind her, she could hear their noise as they made their way home.

Before her on the rock lay a sword, without a scabbard. Its hilt was wrapped in snakeskin—she could see it through the mud. Its blade had a few drops of blood on it. The monkey must have picked it up and it had cut him. She looked around uneasily. Where could it have come from? Had some warrior dropped it? Was he hiding somewhere or lying dead in the stream? She wanted to run like the monkeys and leave it where it lay, but Risu would not move.

Aki bent down warily. Risu gave her an encouraging nudge and she picked up the sword by its hilt. It alarmed her, but at the same time it comforted her. It cleaved to her hand as if it belonged to her. It was a long time since she had held a sword. It reminded her of her father and the training he had given her secretly, at Rinrakuji, so no one would know the girl they called the Autumn Princess could fight with a sword, like a man.

Now that Aki held the sword, Risu was happy to follow her, walking so close she almost stepped on her.

It must be Lord Kiyoyori's sword, Aki thought. *His spirit recognizes it. As soon as the mare saw it the foal quickened.* She was shivering despite the warmth of the sun. The sword had been recast and repaired, but by whom? Why had the stag been at the stream? Was Shikanoko nearby? Was he alive or dead? Was it longing or fear that made her tremble?

She walked swiftly back to the cave, stopping on the way at the bamboo grove and cutting a length of bamboo to act as a scabbard. She washed the sword clean of mud and blood and slipped it into the scabbard, attaching it with a cord she wove from kudzu vine and strips of bark.

The old matriarch, Ame, watched her carefully, but kept her distance, as did all the monkeys. The sword frightened them. Aki tore one of her underrobes into wide strips and wound one of them around her head, covering her face except for her eyes. With the others she bound her legs so the saddle would not chafe them. Then she strapped the lute to the mare's back, saddled Nyorin, and, using a tree stump, climbed onto him.

She bowed her head to Ame and said aloud, "Thank you for everything."

The old monkey sat impassively, her child at her breast, as Aki rode away from the Darkwood, back to the world of swords and horses and men.

7

YOSHI

Yoshi was told to walk, his hands tied in front of him, the rope held by the oldest man, who carried one of the monkeys, Shiro, wrapped up like a bundle, on his shoulder. The other man held Kemuri, while the boy followed with the decoy, holding the cord attached to its collar in his left hand. The monkey gamboled happily, turning somersaults, jumping onto the boy's shoulder, then down to the ground again, chattering all the time.

Shiro and Kemuri screeched in rage and fear and tried to bite and scratch, but the men did not grow angry with them, just laughed in amusement, preventing the monkeys from hurting them, or themselves, with practiced gentleness.

The boy made monkey noises, the kind of sounds an older male might make to young ones, slightly threatening but mostly reassuring. Yoshi began to trust him.

They followed the same path to the edge of the forest that Yoshi had taken with Aki and the horses and came to the old hut and the place at the stream's edge where he thought Shikanoko was going to cut off his head. He couldn't help shivering. There was no sign of Shikanoko. Maybe he was still alive. Or maybe the horses had killed him, after all, and wolves had carried away his bones. He wasn't sure if that made him sad or not. Shikanoko had saved him and Akihime from the men, who he knew were going to do something bad to them, and Yoshi had liked him then, but Shikanoko had been prepared to kill him with the same sudden ruthlessness, and liking had turned to distrust. He knew his father was dead, which was why he was now emperor, though he must never tell anyone, and his mother was dead, too, and Akihime's father and mother, and probably everyone he had ever known, except Akihime and Kai. He felt sorry for them all; he wanted no one else to die, ever.

In the same cave from which Risu and Nyorin had come galloping, the monkey hunters had left a packhorse with two baskets, and another smaller basket, which contained fruit, loquats and apricots. The boy fetched water from the stream in a bamboo flask, put his hands together and said a prayer over it, and gave it to Yoshi so he could drink. Then he fed him fruit, cutting small slices with a sharp knife and putting them in his mouth. The other men did the same with Shiro and Kemuri, holding them on their laps.

The monkeys were not so distressed that they could not

eat; indeed, the food calmed them and they allowed the men to put them on the horse, one in each basket. Yoshi was lifted onto the horse's back, where he sat between the baskets, gripping the mane with his tied hands.

It must have been quite dark inside the baskets, for Shiro and Kemuri went quiet, as if they had fallen asleep. The boy walked beside the packhorse, the tame monkey on his shoulder, and told Yoshi the names of everything they saw, rock, stream, tree, sky, speaking slowly and clearly as if he were teaching him. After a while Yoshi repeated a word, *horse*, and the boy shouted in delight.

"He can talk! He can talk!"

Yoshi continued to say the words after him, and there was something quite funny about learning to speak again, not in the polite, complicated language of the court, but in the direct slang of the riverbank people. He started laughing with every word, and the boy laughed, too, and then the men joined in, feeding him words he suspected were rude, *arse*, *cock*, *balls*. Saying them made him feel like a different person, stronger and older.

"Sarumaru," the boy said, pointing at his own nose. "My name is Sarumaru."

"Kinmaru," the older man said, and the younger one, "Monmaru."

"Yoshi." He could not point to himself as his hands were tied, but he bobbed his head up and down.

"We will call you Yoshimaru." The boy laughed. "We all have children's names. We don't cut our hair, we never grow up. We are children of the road."

Yoshi liked the sound of that. He remembered seeing Sarumaru at Majima and wanting to be him. All the time he had been practicing acrobatics in the forest with the wild monkeys and the two horses, he had been pretending he was that boy. Now he had met him, and was going to live with him. He was young enough to believe in the magic of his own thinking. It made him laugh again.

"Children of God," Monmaru said, and drew something quickly in the air with his index finger. The others murmured as if they were saying a prayer.

They traveled on through the day, resting in the shade for a while when it was hottest. Yoshi's hands were untied then and, afterward, no one seemed to think they should be tied again. There were few people on the road, though they saw farmers in the distance working in the fields, bringing in beans and rice. Most of the paddies were already harvested, and crows gathered in them, picking up every last grain, every insect left exposed. Herons stalked on the banks, looking for frogs. Now and then Yoshi caught a glimpse of gold and black plumage and knew the werehawk was following him. He was not altogether happy about it. Kon was too closely connected with his former life and knew who he really was. Though most people would not understand the werehawk, maybe someone would, maybe the Prince Abbot, who, Yoshi knew, was his most dangerous enemy.

In the afternoon they came to the crossroads where the ghost had not let Risu and Nyorin go any farther, and Shikanoko had summoned it back from the shores of the river of death and into the foal. He remembered the mask, how it had transformed Shikanoko into a supernatural being. He shivered again.

"Usually we would go from here to Rinrakuji," Sarumaru said. "The monks there always used to welcome us and watch our performance. Then they would give us food and shelter. They were good people and truly devout. But the temple was burned by the Miboshi in the early summer and has not been rebuilt."

"And when it is rebuilt the Prince Abbot will install his monks there and bring it under the sway of Ryusonji," Kinmaru said gloomily. "The Prince Abbot does not approve of us or our monkey brothers."

It will never occur to him to look for me among them, Yoshi thought.

That night they camped under the stars. Yoshi was used to this—he often slept in a tree with Shiro and Kemuri and he loved being outside at night, listening to the insects and the night birds, talking to the rabbit in the moon, and gazing at the vast sweep of stars, wondering why some shone more brightly than others, where they went in the day, what lay behind the dome of the sky.

Monmaru lit a fire of green wood and fragrant leaves to keep away mosquitoes. It was only partly effective, the insects whined around their heads, but none of the three tried to swat them. They either brushed them away or watched them as they pierced the skin to suck blood.

"So does the Secret One feed us," Kinmaru said, and again Monmaru drew the sign in the air.

"We have taken a vow not to kill," Sarumaru whispered to Yoshi later. "All beings desire to live, just as we do, and the Secret One has a plan for each life. Who are we to interfere? Our deaths, and everyone else's, are ordained by him and already written in his book. If we interfere with that, we are destroying the harmony and beauty of his great design and letting evil into the world.

"Men fight and kill endlessly. When they are not engaged in battle, great lords hunt for sport, taking thousands of birds and animals in a single day, decking themselves out in the plumage and fur of the slaughtered, fletching their shafts of death with feathers taken from the dead, so heron kills heron, pheasant, pheasant. Even monks and priests, who claim to follow the Enlightened One, kill for their esoteric rituals, using monkeys' skulls and wolves' hearts. But there is another kingdom, alongside this world in the midst of which we live, both within and without it, where there is no killing, no blood-soaked earth. By refusing to take life, we bring it into being."

Yoshi listened, without saying anything, but in his heart he knew it was in this kingdom that he wanted to live.

"You understand everything, don't you?" Sarumaru said.

Shiro and Kemuri whimpered in their baskets. Sarumaru's monkey, whom he called Tomo, sat next to them, occasionally pushing a piece of fruit under the lid, chattering to them reassuringly. Yoshi wondered if they would ever trust Tomo, after he had deceived them so shamelessly. He had seen the monkeys in the forest outwit one another, either in play or to steal a piece of food, but he had not expected one of them to dissemble so successfully, at the command of a human.

He nodded in reply to Sarumaru's question and smiled tentatively at him.

"So, you haven't lived with the monkeys all your life? You were brought up among people. Where did you come from?"

"I don't remember," Yoshi said.

"I was brought up in the village of Iida," Sarumaru said. He didn't seem tired at all; he was prepared to chat all night. "My family sold me to the acrobats when I was a child. I don't remember much about it. I had a lot of brothers, some older, some younger. Everyone blamed me for everything; they would take it in turns to give me a beating. I tried to run away, I remember that, but someone always came after me, my father or my older brothers, and then I would get two beatings, one on the spot and one when I got home. I still cried when I left. I didn't know any better. But Mon and Kin have always been kind to me, and now Tomo is my best friend. People laugh when we perform together; they love our act. And when I hear them clap, I'm saying to my brothers in my heart, 'You couldn't do this in a thousand years!'"

"You must forgive them," Kinmaru said.

"Mmm, I do forgive them, but I can't help feeling pleased all the same."

"Stop chattering and let us get some sleep," Monmaru said wearily.

Saru gave an exaggerated sigh and seemed to fall asleep, but a little later he said suddenly, "My oldest brother was very clever. He could use an abacus and even read and write a little. He went to Miyako and worked in the house of a great lord. But I don't know what happened to him after that. One day I'll go and find him and I'll say, 'Look, older brother, Taro, look what I can do. You never imagined that back in Iida, did you?' "

"Go to sleep!" the two older men said simultaneously, and then both laughed.

"Come here, Tomo," Saru said, and, clasping the uncomplaining monkey in his arms, he settled down. With his other arm he pulled Yoshi close to him. He did not say anymore, awake, but Yoshi heard him call out in his dreams.

Two days later they came to Aomizu, where Aki and Yoshi had said goodbye to Kai and the women of the boats, at the end of the third month. He had thought about Kai every day since then and wondered if he would meet her again now, hoping he would, hoping she would not give him away, but he couldn't see any of the beautifully decorated boats or the musicians or the elegant lady who had talked to him so strangely about pollution.

They went to a house by the lakeside where the other monkeys of the troupe had been left, in a yard at the back. Some women lived there—perhaps they were the older men's wives, though Yoshi never really knew for sure—with three or four very young children. The house was noisy; the women shouted and sometimes burst into song, the babies

111

cried, the toddlers were always falling over and sobbing, the monkeys screamed from their enclosure, especially when they saw the new arrivals.

Shiro and Kemuri were kept in a separate cage. They moped and fretted, and Yoshi spent a lot of time with them, comforting them and feeding them tidbits. There always seemed to be plenty of these; the acrobats received many gifts for their performances, and the merchant guild, which oversaw the markets around the lake, provided the house and looked after the families.

Gifts were of food and rice wine, lengths of cloth, gold statues, lacquer bowls, and sometimes even copper coins, which no one was quite sure what to do with. They seemed magical and slightly dangerous in their power to transform goods and transfer ownership. They were usually buried in the yard, as a charm to keep the monkeys safe.

But despite the charms and the tidbits, Yoshi worried about Shiro and Kemuri. "They're so sad," he said to Sarumaru. "They want to go back to the forest. We should take them back."

"It's good that they are sad," Saru said. "That way they'll come to depend on you and me, and that makes them easier to train. They'll get over it; they'll forget their old life and this will be all they know."

Like me, Yoshi thought. Already memories of his early childhood were fading. Perhaps he really had died on the riverbank, and now he had been reborn into a new life. Nothing seemed real before the morning when Shikanoko had intended to kill him, the horses had saved his life, and he had lived in the forest with Akihime and the monkeys.

The acrobats had traveled throughout the summer, attending the great festivals as well as the fifth-day markets, held on the fifth, fifteenth, and twenty-fifth of each month. Now as the typhoon season began they stayed close to home, training the new monkeys and practicing with the old.

Training was slow, but the men and Saru were patient. They were never cruel, though they would reprimand any misbehavior with a sharp word or a tap on the culprit's paw, just as they did with the toddlers, who, Yoshi saw, were also being trained to learn the same tricks and be as attentive and obedient. Shiro and Kemuri were smarter than the children and learned more quickly. This seemed to please them, and they began to seek rewards and to treat the toddlers like younger, less intelligent monkeys, with a mixture of concern and scorn.

They still squealed with delight and ran to cling to Yoshi whenever they saw him, but they also came to love Sarumaru, as all the monkeys did. They competed for his attention and tried to please him, not only for the rewards but for his words of praise, the way he scratched their heads and let them climb all over him.

Saru developed an act where he would appear among the crowd, covered in monkeys, a walking fur creature with six faces. Children ran screaming, as if from an ogre, only to run back in delight as Saru peeled off the monkeys, one by one, and sent them somersaulting into the air.

The first typhoon of the year came roaring across the lake, dumping rivers of rain from its dark, heavy clouds, turning day to night, flooding the roads around the lake, and tearing roofs from the flimsy dwellings. When it was over everyone set to, cheerfully, to dry out clothes and bedding, repair houses, clean mud from walls and floors. Typhoons were a part of life, to be dealt with like everything else, with the mixture of good humor, patience, and gratitude that was the acrobats' way.

At the end of the ninth month, when the storms had cleared and the fine weather of autumn had set in, they began to get ready to take to the road again. The monkeys were excited; the women seemed sad and relieved at the same time; the children cried because they wanted to go, too. Saru told Yoshi they would take him, Shiro, and Kemuri.

"We will go down to the Rainbow Bridge for the fifth-day market, then back here for the fifteenth. That way, if you don't like it, or the new monkeys get upset by the crowds, you can stay here with them until we come back for the winter."

"I will like it," Yoshi said, "I know I will."

"You have to be prepared for anything, think on your feet, turn a bad situation into something good. All eyes are on you: people waiting for you to make them laugh, many hoping you will fail so they can jeer at you. It takes a bit of getting used to. And sometimes the monkeys just don't want to perform. They are in a bad mood or they don't feel well, it's windy or the crowd is hostile. Then you have to make the best of that as well, not freeze up or show that you're flustered."

"You make it sound hard, but it looks so easy," Yoshi said.

"Wait till you see me in a real crowd," Saru boasted.

Yoshi opened his mouth to say he already had, at Majima, but then he thought better of it. He did not want to say anything about his past. He just wanted to be the boy who had grown up with the monkeys.

That night the old man who had visited the women's boat, the day Akihime and he had left it, came to the house to share the evening meal. Yoshi pretended he hadn't seen him before, but he remembered him well and all the things he had said. He kept his head lowered and stayed at the back of the circle. The old man prayed before the start of the meal, the others responding in low, reverent voices. Then he served food to each of them, as he had done before, as though he were one of the women, not an old priest who deserved respect. Yoshi felt the old man's keen eyes on him, but he did not speak to him until the end of the meal, when he began to say the words of blessing for the departure.

Kinmaru, Monmaru, and Saru, who were leaving the next day, shuffled forward and knelt before him. Saru reached out behind him and pulled Yoshi alongside them.

"He is coming with us," he said. "And he needs blessing more than anyone, for he is alone in the world, apart from us."

Yoshi knelt, keeping his head down, and felt the old man's hands rest lightly on his hair.

"May the Secret One guide you always," he said quietly. "You have taken a different path from the one set out for you, but it will lead you back to the same place, in the end."

I hope not, Yoshi thought. *I want to be a monkey boy like Saru. I don't want to be emperor.*

8

SHIKANOKO

"If you wait for winter to be over, months will be lost," Kongyo said to Shikanoko. "But act now and take Kuma-yama and it will be you the snows protect."

He had made the same argument several times since he had arrived at the hut and found Shika and the boys there. "You are not going to stay in the forest forever. You may as well leave now. Besides, we cannot survive another winter in Kuromori. We must either escape or take our own lives. You would have us fighting for you, seventy men."

"Half-starved," Shika said, with scorn.

"Desperate and capable of anything. Hungry not only for food but, even more, to avenge Lord Kiyoyori." Kongyo clutched his belly. The hare meat had been too rich for him and had given him the gripes. He had had to dash off into the bushes several times and now his face was pale and, despite the chill of the winter afternoon, sweaty.

"You're in no condition to travel," Shika said. "Rest

another day. Let your horse recover, too. I will discuss your suggestion with the boys."

He wondered what Kongyo made of them. The older man had seen them all now, though he could not tell them apart. He had expressed surprise to Shika that they looked so ordinary. They had lost the striking beauty of their early months and now resembled the thin, half-grown boys found in any small village of the Eight Islands. It pleased Shika. He could see it made them less conspicuous. They had become unremarkable. They blended into the forest and he was sure they would blend into any surroundings in the same way.

"I think I will lie down," Kongyo said, "but not in that accursed hut." Cold had driven him the previous night to sleep there among the skulls, masks, and bones, the animal skins and the feather cloaks, but he complained of nightmares the next morning.

"The hut is not accursed," Mu said. "It is something you don't understand, but there is no need to fear it."

The warrior looked astonished to be addressed in this familiar way.

"Nightmares are messages from the gods, like dreams, like the one you yourself said you had," Mu said. "You should be grateful for them. No harm will come to you, unless Shikanoko commands it. Go and lie down inside. It's too cold out here. Ku will keep you company and the dogs will keep you warm."

Shika was surprised by Mu's words, too. They were more than he had ever heard Mu say at one time and there was something strange about them. He realized Mu was copying Kongyo's intonation and vocabulary, as though he were absorbing them directly from the older man's brain. The boys were like the forest leeches, the tiny monsters that Shisoku, and now Kuro, tried in vain to replicate, that sucked blood and consumed earthworms whole.

Ku led Kongyo into the hut, followed by two real dogs and three fake ones. After a few moments the boy came out again and joined Kiku by the fire.

"He is lying down," he said, "but he needs to sleep to get better."

Kiku was boiling something in an iron pot; it smelled of aniseed and rhubarb root.

He took the pot from the embers and poured the contents into a small cup. He handed it to Ku. "Give him this. It will settle his stomach and send him to sleep."

"You aren't planning to poison our guest, I hope," Shika said.

"Of course not," Kiku replied, adding, "I will if you want me to."

"Thank you," Shika said. "I'm pleased to see you all being so considerate."

"If he is soundly asleep, you can discuss your plans freely with us," Kiku replied. "We are not being considerate, we are being practical."

"We are learning a lot from him, too," Mu remarked. "What did he mean when he said *avenge*?"

"It is when you want to harm or punish someone who has injured you. Payback. It is a sort of justice."

Mu considered this reply for a few moments. Then he said, "Who was Lord Kiyoyori?"

"He was a great warrior; they called him the Kuromori lord. Kuromori is the fortress where our guest, Kongyo, has been hiding out." After a pause Shika said quietly, "He was one of your fathers."

"As well as Shisoku?" Kiku had been listening carefully to every word. The boys knew nothing of normal human relations, so they accepted this more or less unquestioningly.

"You had five fathers: Shisoku; Kiyoyori; a bandit chief, Akuzenji; a great sage and magician, Sesshin; and me."

Kiku and Mu both laughed.

"You are very young to be our father," Mu said. "Aren't you?"

"You are our older brother," Kiku added.

"I am old enough to make children," Shika said. "And, I suppose, the way you are growing, you soon will be, too."

The boys were silent while they thought about this. They were both smiling. Kiku gave Mu a shove; Mu punched him back.

Something else I will have to teach them about, Shika thought. *But who will they marry? Will they take human wives? And what will become of their children?*

"Do you want to avenge Lord Kiyoyori, too?" Mu asked.

"I do, and I will. But first I need to kill my uncle," Shika replied, and thought, *And then I have to destroy the Prince Abbot, and*—he hardly dared to put his longing into words, even silent ones—*find Akihime and marry her, and restore Yoshimori to the throne.* Kumayama was the first step toward all these goals.

"This is Kumayama, where my uncle lives now." He picked up a charred stick and began to draw a rough map on one of the firestones. "This is where I grew up."

He was suddenly besieged by memories, the daily humiliations and cruelties, the helpless rages he had fallen into, when everything went red and he wanted only to lash out, to kill and destroy, the sense of outrage and injustice that the man who was supposed to care for him, who held his inheritance in trust, wanted him dead and was driving him either to suicide or to an act so uncontrolled, it would justify his execution.

He was deeply grateful he had fallen over the cliff, grateful to the stag that had cushioned his fall and to the men who had spared his life and in their own strange way nurtured and educated him: Shisoku, Akuzenji, Kiyoyori, Sesshin. They had all been like fathers to him, so, in a sense, he was the boys' older brother.

He became aware they were watching him, the stick still in his hand, waiting for him to go on. He said, "I was there briefly a year ago. I was a prisoner, so I could not see how my uncle had changed and fortified my old home since I had been away—it is nearly two years ago now."

Kiku said, "Explain *uncle*."

"My father's brother. If Mu had a child, you would be the uncle."

This made them laugh again. Kiku dug Mu in the ribs with his elbow. "Who is your child's mother going to be?

One of those bitches you sleep with? Your children will be puppies!"

Mu hit him and they tumbled over on top of Gen, waking him from sleep. He leaped to his feet, snarling and snapping. Shika silenced all three with a look, and went on. "This is how it was when I lived there—we called it a castle, but really it was just a fortified house, with a high wooden fence around it, a ditch in front of the fence, strong gates at front and rear, and a watchtower. Just inside the rear gate are cells with wooden bars, and between them and the house is an open space where horses are exercised, and where anyone who annoys my uncle is put to death."

He moved on to the adjacent stone. "The stable is also at the rear. It's an open shed with ropes for the horses to be tied to. Fodder and water buckets are stored here. The roofs are all thatch, reeds, not bones."

"It looks interesting," Mu said. "It's so big!"

"Yet it is small compared with many other fortresses," Shika said. "Small but very important. Difficult to take, easy to defend."

"I'd like to see it for myself," Kiku said.

"I hope you will soon. Now leave me in peace for a while."

Shika went to the hut, saw that Kongyo was deeply asleep, and took the shoulder blades of the stag from where they lay on the altar. He had found them among Gessho's possessions after the monk's death. He said a few words of prayer over them and placed them in the embers of the fire. Then he sat cross-legged, meditating, until the sun set.

At nightfall he took the cooled blades from the ashes and studied the fine hairlike cracks that had appeared on them. He felt he heard their message in his own bones.

Kongyo did not wake, but that night his horse became colicky from the sudden large amounts of food it had eaten so hungrily, and, despite Shika's efforts to save it, died in the early hours of the morning. As soon as Ima woke and saw the dead horse, he set about skinning it. The head and hooves were buried, like Gessho's skull, to rot away the flesh. The mane and tail were cut off and given to Ku, who washed them carefully and combed them out, so they regained in death the rippled silkiness they had lost in life. The dogs and wolves sat around, mouths dripping strings of saliva. When the belly was slit open Ima threw the still-steaming entrails to them and they snapped and fought over them.

Shika reread the message in the shoulder blades.

"I am going to Kumayama," he informed Kongyo. "If you're well enough to ride, you can take my horse. Return to Kuromori and tell your men to expect me. I suppose I will be there in about ten days. If I'm not, you can assume either we are snowed in or I have failed. Your future will be in your own hands then."

"You will not fail," Kongyo said, his eyes gleaming. "We have my dream to trust in."

"You're taking us with you, aren't you?" Mu said.

"Are we going to kill the uncle?" Kiku asked.

"Do you want to?" said Shika.

Kiku looked around at the bone-thatched hut, the animals assembled from various parts of corpses, the carcass of the dead horse, and said, "I don't mind."

The middle boy, Kuro, emerged from the forest carrying a pole across his shoulders from which hung several small bamboo cages. He set them carefully on the ground and crouched down, his eyes fixed on his oldest brother.

"What have you got there?" Shika asked.

"A giant centipede, two golden orb spiders, a viper, and a very angry sparrow bee," Kuro replied.

Kongyo shuddered. "I would rather face a hundred Miboshi warriors than any one of those—apart from the snake. Snakes are easy to kill, you just lop off their head."

"This one is half-asleep," Kuro interrupted him. "It will not wake up properly till spring."

Kongyo ignored him. "But insects! You don't see them until it's too late. They lie in wait in dark corners and shadowy places, and they sting and bite without discrimination or mercy."

"Are all warriors cowards when it comes to insects?" Kiku said. The question sounded innocent, but Shika knew Kiku intended to insult Kongyo and unsettle him.

"It is not a question of cowardice," Kongyo began.

Shika held up a hand to calm him. "We will find out." A plan was beginning to form in his mind. "Kiku and Kuro will come with me. Mu, you will stay with Ima and Ku."

"I'd rather go with you," Mu pleaded.

Shika did not want the two older boys squabbling and competing, leading each other into danger. Kuro was the most solitary, usually, but he had more respect for Kiku than Mu did, and his poisonous insects could be useful. "I'm trusting you to look after your brothers and the animals. You must be what Shisoku was, the guardian of this place, of the forest."

This seemed to placate Mu a little, and he was smiling as he went away from them and joined Ima, who was now slicing strips of flesh from the dead horse and threading them on sharpened sticks. Mu began to place these on forked poles above a bed of embers. Shika hoped the weather stayed fine. If the meat dried quickly, it would feed the boys for half the winter.

The sparrow bee had found it could not escape and was buzzing furiously against the narrow bamboo bars. Kongyo looked at it, fascinated and horrified.

"Lord Kiyoyori's brother, Masachika, was half-dead from what he said were bee stings when we found him after the attack. He told us they had stung him on the orders of the guardian spirits at Matsutani. I thought he was hallucinating, but maybe they were giant bees like this one."

"He would not be half-dead but all dead," Kuro replied. "But there are many kinds of bees, wasps, and hornets, and many different levels of poison."

"Aren't you afraid they'll sting you? Then you'd be all dead!" Kongyo laughed, but no one else did.

"I let them sting me," Kuro said. "I am immune now." He flashed a look at Kongyo from his expressionless eyes. Sometimes, Shika thought, the boys looked like insects themselves, and he recalled how they had been born from eggs in cocoons, like spiders.

※

Kongyo left at dawn the next day, and shortly afterward Shika, Kiku, and Kuro set out for Kumayama. Shika took his bow and Jinan, and the mask, in the seven-layered brocade bag, together with the shoulder blades of divination. The boys took knives, ropes, bows and venom-tipped arrows, and other poisons, carefully sealed with stoppers of beeswax in bamboo tubes, and the sparrow bee in its cage. It had gone silent and Shika thought it was dead, but Kuro assured him it was sleeping; he had blown a drowse smoke over it and could waken it when it was needed. Gen, the fake wolf, came with them, inseparable as always from Shika.

They moved silently and swiftly through the winter forest. In low, shady places the ground was white with frost. Most of the trees were leafless, only pines and cedars still deep green. Kuro said after a while, "Will that man let our horse die of hunger, too?"

"It may happen, though I hope not," Shika replied.

"If the horse was hungry, why didn't it run away and find food?"

"I expect it was tied up, somewhere inside the fortress. Horses suffer along with men in war. They are killed in battle, they starve in sieges." Shika found himself thinking of Risu and Nyorin, and the foal. The time of its birth must be getting close. He wondered what would happen when it was born, if he would ever see it, ever know if Kiyoyori's spirit truly dwelled within it.

"And then they get eaten," Kiku added.

Kuro said, "Do men get eaten, too?"

"Sometimes, I believe, starving, desperate people will eat the flesh of a dead human being, but generally not."

"Why do horses submit to men? Why do they let themselves be tamed? I would never do that!" Kuro declared.

"I suppose it is in their nature," Shika replied. "Something in them longs to be mastered. When they submit, they feel safe. Most horses don't get to choose their owners. They are passed from hand to hand. If a new owner treats them properly, and feeds them, they obey and are content. There are many people like that in the world, you will find. They are happy to obey. But, like horses, while most will follow, a few others always want to be in front."

"It is not in *our* nature to follow," Kiku said.

Shika laughed. "I don't believe it is. Yet you and Mu are leaders over your brothers, and you all obey me, and must, until you are fully grown and understand how the world works."

"Who do you follow?" Kuro asked.

"No one," Shika said, after a pause. "I am the horse that wants to go first."

"What happens when several horses all want to be in front?" Kiku said.

"They jostle and nip one another. Eventually they fight."

"So, you are going to do a little jostling and nipping against your uncle?" said Kiku. "And then you will fight?"

"Exactly."

On the evening of the fourth day they came to a place Shika remembered, at the foot of a steep cliff. He found the stag's skeleton, and marveled that wolves had not scattered the bones. He helped the boys build a rough shelter a short distance away, and shared out the last of the food they had brought with them.

It was hardly enough to satisfy their hunger. Kuro set traps for rabbits and then declared he was going to forage for nuts and mushrooms. Shika told Kiku to keep watch and went back to the place where he had come tumbling down the cliff, expecting to die. The stag had broken his fall, and in saving his life changed it beyond imagination. Now he wanted to thank it, he needed to tell the mountain, Kumayama, he was back, and he wanted to test the power of the mask.

Kneeling beside the skeleton, he placed the mask over his face, prepared to face the Prince Abbot, should he be taken into his presence, and to remove the mask swiftly if he had to. It was more than a month since Gessho had died, and, even though the werehawk messenger had been killed, too, surely the priest would have divined what had happened by now?

Shika breathed in and out slowly, bringing his thoughts under control. Little by little, his mind quieted, and he felt his spiritual power awaken. He was aware of everything around him. He could feel the forest in its deep winter sleep, he knew its dreams. He spoke to it and to the mountain, thanking them both for sustaining him, seeking their protection. Then he spoke to the stag. He saw it tread proudly through the forest, its antlers held erect, its nose twitching, its eyes bright. He heard its autumn cry of yearning and loneliness. He expressed his sorrow at its death, his gratitude for all it had done for him. He called it Father and told it his name, Shikanoko, the deer's child.

He felt no sign of the power of the Prince Abbot, nor was he taken into the realm of Ryusonji. The mask had been broken, he had been broken, but, in the mending, they had both become stronger.

He rose to his feet and began the movements of the deer dance. For a while he was transported by it. He thought he saw inside Kumayama, his uncle made cruel by his fear of attack from without and rebellion from within. He saw the fortress weighed down by hatred and repression; one push and it would fall. He saw the two great lords, the leaders of the Miboshi and the Kakizuki; he realized he could become greater than either of them. Kongyo's dream came into his mind as though he had dreamed it himself. He straddled the Eight Islands. He would put the rightful emperor on the throne and rule through him.

But then his feet faltered. He did not know the rest of the movements, he had never learned all the steps. And now Shisoku was gone, there was no one to teach him. In that moment of doubt, he felt the pull of Ryusonji, as though the Prince Abbot had woken and turned his attention to the east. He felt a surge of longing and regret. He saw all the wisdom and knowledge that dwelled at Ryusonji and longed to be part of it again. He missed the admiration and affection he had so often heard in the Prince Abbot's voice. He wanted to hear that voice again at the same time as he cringed from it.

He felt the bound beginning, as it had before, the stag's leap that would take him there in minutes. He would not go inside, he would just stand on the veranda . . .

He tore the mask from his face, his heart pounding.

That night he hardly dared sleep, lest he should meet his former master in his dreams. Instead his thoughts circled and returned over and again to all he needed to learn.

In the morning there were two rabbits in Kuro's traps. They skinned and cooked them, fed the entrails to Gen, ate one, and took the other with them. The boys scaled the cliff easily, thanks to their skills in balance and leaping. They let down a rope for Shika to climb. Then the three followed the route along which he and his uncle had tracked the stag, two years before. He was in familiar territory now—he had roamed over this mountain as a boy, and, though there were no paths and it looked as if no one had been here in the past two years, they made swift progress. Did his uncle no longer hunt in this part of the mountain? Was he afraid he might meet Kazumaru's angry ghost?

The boys went ahead, for they could move more silently than Shika, and Kiku's sharp hearing would warn them of anyone in their path. They slept briefly for two nights, not making fires, sharing the rabbit, cracking and sucking the bones, then huddling together against the cold. Shika noticed that Gen's body, once as chill as the elements he was made of, now gave out a natural warmth.

Around midday on the third day Gen sniffed the air and said indistinctly, "Dead people."

At the same time Kiku appeared.

"There's a strange noise ahead," he reported. "Flapping and rustling."

"Can you hear that noise, Gen?" Shika whispered.

The fake wolf turned his head and pricked the right ear, which had always worked better than the left.

"Birds," he said.

As they cautiously approached the source of the noise, Shika saw Gen was right. A flock of crows swarmed over some thing, or things, mounted on poles. The birds did not caw, or even squabble. They simply pecked, relentlessly and silently, every now and then fluttering up into the air and then returning.

At the sight of Shika and the boys, they flew off into nearby trees, where they made the boughs hang down heavily, and watched with greedy, inquisitive eyes.

The things heaved and swayed, as if they still lived, but it was not life within them but life feeding on them. Countless maggots teemed over them.

"That's a head," Kuro said with interest. "And those must have been internal organs. You can still see their shape and texture."

"Not so unlike an animal's," Kiku said, equally fascinated. "There is the heart, liver, kidneys, and look, even the private parts!"

They both laughed callously. "Still with a mind of their own," Kiku said. "Even in death."

One of the crows cawed, breaking the silence. Gen growled and snapped at it.

"Is this the sort of thing your uncle does?" Kuro asked.

"This looks like his work," Shika replied.

"No wonder you hate him."

Kiku said quietly, "It takes many years to grow to a man, doesn't it? Many times longer than for us?"

Shika nodded. This man had been an adult. What remained of his hair suggested he might have been forty years old: forty years of human life, with all its complexities and intricacies, reduced to slabs of meat exposed in the forest, food for grubs and crows.

"Who was he? Did you know him?"

There was nothing to identify the dead man. Sademasa had many retainers and even more farmers, from whom he extracted tax in produce and labor. It could be any one of them, executed and dishonored in death. How fragile were even the strongest of men.

"Can you find out?" Kiku persisted.

"How do you suggest I do that?" Shika said.

"You could use that mask, in the bag," Kiku said.

"How do you know about that?"

"I saw you, the night before we climbed the cliff. And I've watched you before, at the hut. You put it on and go into some other place. Do it now."

"Kiku's got a plan," Kuro said, smiling in glee, seeming to read his brother's thoughts.

"We could tease your uncle a little," Kiku said. "Make it easier for you to kill him."

With some reluctance, Shika took the mask from the brocade bag. The crows cawed wildly and flew up in one dark cloud. He prayed briefly, steeling his mind against his former master, and placed it against his face. He found himself on the bank of the river of death, as when he had met Kiyoyori's spirit. He saw again the deep, dark water and heard the splash of oars. Then he heard someone call out to him, in anguish and relief, using his childhood name.

"Kazumaru! Help me!"

"Who are you?"

"I am Naganori, your friend's father."

Shika's throat closed up in horror and pity. His eyes were hot. He forced himself to speak. "What happened to you? Where is Nagatomo? Is he dead, too?"

"He was still alive when I died. Sademasa, your uncle, made him watch my agony and humiliation. My love and fear for my son has bound me to this place. I cannot cross the river until I know his fate, and until we are both avenged. My lord, Kazumaru, make your uncle pay. Make him suffer as so many have. People long for your return. Many of us regretted not helping you last year. We all knew who you were. Can you ever forgive us?"

"I will when my uncle is dead and I hold Kumayama," Shika replied.

"Most of your house still consider themselves Kakizuki. They hate the Miboshi, who are now our overlords. Some of us whispered about it, it was only talk, but we were betrayed. Sademasa has informants everywhere. My punishment was a warning to others."

Shika had less time on this occasion before he felt the Prince Abbot's attention drawn to him. He saw the eyes turn and seek him out. Twice he had aroused the priest now. The Prince Abbot would not ignore such provocation. He would move against him, would send someone else after him. Not a lone monk, but armed warriors, maybe the whole Miboshi army.

"Farewell," he said to Naganori. "Today I will avenge you; Sademasa will die and your son will be saved. If I fail, you and I and Nagatomo will cross the river together."

He took the mask from his face. The boys were watching him with more than usual respect, their black eyes wide and gleaming.

"How much did you see and hear?" Shika asked.

"We heard everything," Kiku replied. "We must go at once and save your friend's life."

"That's a good thing, isn't it?" Kuro questioned.

"Of course it is!" Kiku gave him a cuff on the ear.

Kuro frowned. "Sometimes I'm not sure when it's right to kill and when it's right to save a life."

"Trust Shikanoko," Kiku said. "Just kill anyone he says."

"Feel free to get rid of someone who's attacking me, even if I haven't specifically told you to!" Shika said, as they began to run.

"I just hope I don't get it wrong." Kuro sounded unusually worried.

"It doesn't matter much," Kiku assured him. "Everyone dies in the end."

The fortress stood on the slopes of Kumayama, overlooking a long finger-shaped valley, through which ran the Kumagawa. On either side of the river, on every inch of flat land and on terraces cut out of the hillside, rice was grown, but all the fields were bare now, covered in their winter blankets of mulch, dead leaves, and manure, the higher ones white with frost.

Shika, Kiku, and Kuro came down Kumayama at dawn and hid themselves in thick bushes, from which they studied the fortress for a long time, without speaking. In the year since Shika had last seen his childhood home, it had been even more heavily fortified, with a new palisade of sharpened logs around it and a higher watchtower on each corner. All cover had been cleared around the palisade and guards stood in the watchtowers and at the gates. All day, groups of men rode on horseback around the open area and set up targets and practiced archery.

Laborers were working on some huge earthmoving project, excavating tons of soil and moving it, bucket load by bucket load, to the farther edge of the clearing. Shika realized they were digging a moat and building ramparts for further defense. He wondered why it would be necessary, now that the land from Miyako all the way to Minatogura was in the hands of the Miboshi. What was his uncle so afraid of? Was the control of the Miboshi not as secure as it appeared? Was Sademasa, like all turncoats, prey to guilt and suspicion? He had certainly made his fortress impregnable.

There were two strange machines on platforms on the ramparts, and any rocks that were uncovered were lugged up to their base and added to the piles amassed there.

"Catapults!" Kuro said. The boys made small ones from strips of leather that they chewed for hours to render pliable.

"Could you get inside?" Shika whispered to Kiku.

"Kuro and I can get in at night," Kiku replied. "We can scale the fence at the corner, jump across to the roof, and burrow through the thatch. No one will see us."

"And then what?" Kuro said.

"Shika goes inside and meets his uncle. While they're talking we'll tease him and unsettle him. Then he gets killed."

"That's more or less what I had in mind," Shika said. "A few details need working out. What about his men? I can't take them all on, single-handed."

"We don't know about them," Kiku said. "They're your concern. You deal with them."

"I will be disarmed as soon as I go in," Shika said, thinking aloud. "If I'm not killed immediately. You must take my sword, and get it to me somehow. I'll carry my bow and knife. They will think it strange if I arrive completely unarmed. And I must offer them something they want, so they keep me alive."

They spent the short winter day watching and listening. Shika mapped the fortress as he remembered it and Kiku's sharp hearing enabled him to place its inhabitants within. At the end of the day, Sademasa rode out to inspect the earthworks. They could all hear him clearly as he shouted at the foremen, complaining about the slow progress and the poor quality. His face lit up as he saw the piles of rocks and the catapults. He went to the nearest machine, dismounted, and caressed its throwing arm, which was tied down, with a rock loaded in place. Then he peered down the valley, as if assessing how far the rock would be hurled.

Kiku and Kuro watched him with bright eyes. Shika's hand gripped his bow, but his uncle was beyond its reach, and anyway wore a helmet and protective leather armor around chest and neck.

"We know him now," Kiku said.

"You could offer him Gen," Kuro suggested.

"Gen?" Shika said, surprised.

The fake wolf whimpered anxiously.

"He likes strange artefacts, man-made devices. Show him Gen and tell him you have the power to make things like this—artificial animals and men. He does not have enough warriors. He needs an army."

Night fell swiftly. There was no moon and the sky was covered with low clouds that threatened snow. Shika made the boys embrace him before they left, and the feel of their thin, scarcely human bodies against his filled him with tenderness. He wondered if they felt the same, if they were like Gen and would grow more real through affection.

He could not see them once they had moved three feet away nor could he hear them. No sound came from the fortress, no clamor as intruders were discovered. The night remained peaceful, bitterly cold.

Shika barely slept. Gen crawled close to him, but could not warm him. By daybreak he was so cold he could hardly walk. He forced himself to stand, to stretch, to run on the spot, in order to get the blood flowing into his extremities. He wondered where the boys were. He could see no sign of entry through the roof. He would have to trust that they were inside.

When he could move freely, he took up the bow and the brocade bag with the mask, slung the quiver with its twelve arrows on his back, and, with Gen at his heels, walked swiftly down to the fortress.

Men were stamping their feet and rubbing their hands together at the gate. Just inside burned a fire in an iron brazier. For a moment Shika thought how appealing the warmth was, and wanted nothing more than to sit by it for a while and thaw out. But he put aside this and all other distractions—hunger, fear, hope, revenge—and concentrated fully on what had to be done to bind the will of those surrounding him to his own.

He called at the gate, "I am Kumayama no Kazumaru, known as Shikanoko, only son of Shigetomo. I have come to pay my respects to your lord, who is also my uncle, and offer him my service and a magic gift."

One of the men moved to the gate and peeked through it. A look of shock crossed his face and he stepped hurriedly back to confer with the others. They spoke quietly, but Shika's hearing, though not as sharp as Kiku's, was keener than most humans' and he could hear them clearly.

"It's that wild boy who turned up last year, claiming to be Kazumaru."

"Are you sure? He was taken away by the Prince Abbot's men to be put to death."

"It's him."

"Kazumaru? He died in the mountains two years ago."

"But he was alive last year. Some people said they recognized him. Naganori, for example."

"Naganori! Look what happened to him!"

"What'll we do?"

Several men came to the gate to peer at him.

"Look at him," said one. "He's a vagabond, been living rough in the forest and wants to get out of the cold. Cut his throat and bury him without saying anything. Save us a mountain of trouble."

"I'm not going to murder the old lord's son," said the man who had first come to the gate.

His name suddenly came back to Shika and he called to him. "Tsunemasa! Let me in and tell my uncle I am here."

Tsunemasa approached the gate, but the man who had wanted to cut Shika's throat pushed him back. "What's the gift?" he said.

"I remember you, Nobuto," Shika said quietly. "I will not forget that you suggested murdering me."

"You'll be praying for my swift knife later today," Nobuto threatened. "When our lord gets you in his hands, whether you are Kazumaru or some vagrant, you'll be begging me to kill you. Show me what the gift is."

"Open the gate and I will," Shika said.

"Who's with you?"

"No one. Just me and my gift."

A man called from the watchtower. "He has come alone."

Nobuto drew back the huge bolts and the gate swung open.

Shika stepped inside and Gen followed him closely, his nose nudging the back of his legs.

"What is that?" Nobuto exclaimed.

Shika was so used to Gen that he had forgotten how strange the fake wolf looked. Now he saw him afresh, the blue gem eyes, the human tongue, the wolf-skin coat through which the skeleton showed.

"This is my gift," he said, feeling Gen quiver. "It is an artificial wolf. I believe my uncle loves all strange devices. I can make these things for him, and more. I can make men."

"I will take the creature to show him," Nobuto said.

"By all means, but I must go with him. He is easily alarmed and quite fierce."

"Wolves don't scare me, alive or not," Nobuto said with a laugh.

"I do not want him destroyed through stupidity or carelessness," Shika said.

Gen snarled, showing his tongue and his artificial teeth. The thick wolf fur on his neck bristled. Nobuto stepped back as the creature lunged at him.

"Wait here," he said. "I will inform the lord."

After Nobuto had left, Tsunemasa said, "Come and sit by the fire, you look frozen." Shika shook his head. He would accept nothing that was his uncle's; he would take it all when the usurper was dead.

He stood just inside the gate without moving. One by one people came out to take a look at him, men and women, warriors and maids, but he did not return their curious stares. With one part of his mind he was wondering where Kiku and Kuro were, but otherwise he was preparing himself for the coming confrontation.

Nobuto finally returned. "My lord will see you and examine your gift. Give me your weapons."

When Shika handed over the bow, the quiver, and the knife, Nobuto looked at the bow carefully and then studied Shika with narrowed eyes. But all he said was, "No sword?"

"A sword is of little use in the forest," Shika replied. "I have not been fighting men for the past two years. But I have been hunting."

"Hmm. What's this?" Nobuto had taken the seven-layered brocade bag that hung at Shika's waist and was opening it.

"It is a mask made from a deer's skull."

"The one the monk was so thrilled to see? You should give this to the lord, too."

"No one can wear it but me. It destroys the face of anyone else who puts it on."

Nobuto closed the bag without looking in it and handed it hurriedly back to Shika. He ran his hands over him to check for any other weapons, opened Shika's mouth and peered inside, pulled at his tangled hair. Shika submitted without emotion. He felt Nobuto's fear, the fear warriors had for anything they did not understand, especially the world of magic and sorcery. And he felt gratitude again that he had been taken out of their world and given the chance to know another, of great richness and strangeness, beyond human imagination. Fate dictated every man's path in life. His uncle's cruelty had been an instrument in his destiny.

For that reason I will give him a swift death, he resolved.

The crowd in the yard parted before him as he followed Nobuto into the fortress, Gen, panting slightly, at his side.

He remembered his old home well, despite the changes that had been made to it—the barred windows, the internal doors that had to be unbolted, at a password, and bolted again behind him. He glimpsed trapdoors and sensed concealed rooms. He thought suddenly of his father, the tengu, and the fateful game of Go. He heard the click and rattle of stones. And then a sharp recollection of his mother, whom he had not seen since he was a child, rose in his mind. Usually, he had only the haziest of memories—the feel of a robe, an outline against an open door—and he had never understood why she had left him, but he suddenly felt assured that she had never forgotten him and that she had been praying for him all this time. It was with a softened heart, then, that he faced his uncle.

Sademasa wore the same armor, leather laced with deep purple cords; his sword lay close to his hand. He sat on a raised platform, with no other concession to comfort or luxury than a thin straw mat. Fifteen retainers were in the reception room with him, five along each side wall, five at the back.

Shika knelt, lowering his head to the ground. Then, after an interval that was not quite respectful or long enough, he sat up and, without waiting to be addressed, said, "I hope you are well, Uncle."

Sademasa was frowning as he answered. "My health is no concern of yours, whoever you are. I am surprised you have dared show your face here again. You must be eager to cross the river of death. I will speed your journey. I can promise you, you will not leave alive this time, even if the Prince Abbot himself should come begging for you."

"There is no need to be hasty," Shika said. "I can do you no injury, alone and unarmed as I am. Maybe I can be of service to you."

Sademasa did not reply immediately, but studied Shika's face intently.

"Stop pretending, Uncle. You must recognize me. You have looked long enough. You know it is I, Kazumaru."

He heard the quick intake of breath from the men surrounding him.

"Kazumaru, alas, is dead," Sademasa said without conviction. "Show me the creature and explain how it works."

Shika pulled the reluctant Gen around and placed him in front of him. Sademasa's eyes narrowed in disbelief.

"What half-aborted monstrosity is this?"

"It is a wolf, but man-made. I have many such creatures and can make many more."

Sademasa said, without hesitation, "Can you make men?"

"Men of a sort," Shika said, lying, for even Shisoku had never attempted a man.

"How? Do you skin the dead, as a wolf was skinned for this, and stuff them with straw?"

"It is the same process." Shika was thinking, *Where are the boys? How long can I keep up this strange conversation?*

"An army of half men," Sademasa said slowly. "That would be something. Can they be taught to fight?"

"The wolf has grown more real," Shika said. Gen snarled at Sademasa's intense stare and showed his teeth. "You see, it snarls, it will bite, it feeds on meat."

"Can it die? Would these men die?"

"They can only be destroyed by fire. Any other damage can be patched up. They are not truly alive, therefore they cannot die."

"Well, I will have this one taken apart so I can see its workings."

Gen gave a sharp howl, and Sademasa leaned forward. "How interesting. It understands every word, doesn't it? I look forward to its dissection. Maybe it will tell me itself how it was made." Sademasa smiled in satisfaction. "Nobuto said you also have the magic mask, the one the monk would not let me see before."

Shika bowed his head. *Kiku! Hurry up or Gen and I will both be dissected!*

"Show it to me," Sademasa commanded.

Shika drew it carefully from the seven-layered bag and held it up with both hands, the face turned to Sademasa. Stillness fell as, one by one, the men in the room became aware of its power. Even Sademasa was silenced. Eventually he said, "Give it to me."

"Uncle, it will burn anyone who tries to wear it, except me."

Sademasa pursed his lips as he considered this.

"Fetch the traitor's son," he ordered, and Nobuto and another retainer left the room. They returned, after a few moments, dragging between them a young man the same age as Shika. It was his childhood friend Nagatomo.

He had been beaten so badly he could not stand. His arms were pinioned behind his back. Blood stained his face and hair. When the men released him he fell to the ground. Nobuto kicked him. He groaned but did not scream.

Shika's heart hardened immediately as horror, pity, and rage filled it.

Sademasa said to Nobuto, "Place the mask on his face and we will see if the vagabond is telling the truth."

"It will burn him," Shika warned again.

Nobuto smiled slightly, as if the prospect amused and pleased him. Sademasa leaned forward with cold curiosity.

Shika rose, intending to throw himself on his uncle and kill him with his bare hands, but two of Sademasa's warriors seized him and held him down.

One retainer held Nagatomo's face upward and Nobuto pressed the mask against it. A scream of such pain erupted from the lips that even the most brutal retainers shuddered. Nagatomo writhed helplessly against the restraining grip. The smell of seared flesh filled the room.

Through the screams Shika heard something else, a voice that sounded like the dead Naganori.

"Sademasa," it called, "I am waiting for you!"

A ripple of shock ran through the room as the men registered the voice, but, before anyone could act, a high-pitched buzzing came from the roof. Shika looked up and saw a crack open in the ceiling and the sparrow bee burst through it.

Naganori's voice called again, "Sademasa!"

Sademasa, distracted by the voice, did not notice the sparrow bee until too late. It flew straight to his face and stung him on the lips. He brushed it aside, and it immediately stung his hand. The men holding Shika let go and rushed forward.

The crack in the ceiling opened wider and through it dropped Shika's sword, Jinan. He was about to snatch the mask from Nagatomo's face, but instead he caught the sword by the hilt and raised it to strike Sademasa. But it was not needed. The venom had already done its work. His uncle was scrabbling at his throat with his hands, gasping for breath, his chest heaving against the tightly laced armor, his eyes bulging. He fell forward, his legs jerked and kicked, he lost control of bowel and bladder and the stench in the room grew worse.

The sparrow bee buzzed angrily as it swooped around, making the retainers shrink from it. One or two of them drew their swords, trying to hit it with the flat of the blade. But they only enraged it further. It had stung two more men, sending them to the same choking death as Sademasa, who now lay unmoving on the floor, before someone thought to unbar the door and the surviving men rushed out.

Shika stood with sword raised, but no one approached him. Then he went to Nagatomo, whose screams had subsided to moans. Shika removed the mask from his face and looked carefully at the damage. Through the scorched skin the eyes stared back at him, reduced by agony to something scarcely human. Yet they saw Shika, and recognized him, and another light came into them.

Shika knelt beside him and gently untied his arms, rubbing the numb fingers as the blood rushed back into them. The eyes wept tears of pain.

"I am sorry," Shika whispered. "Forgive me. You will not die. We will save you."

Kiku and Kuro dropped through the ceiling, restless with delight and triumph. They paid no attention to Nagatomo.

"That went all right, didn't it?" Kiku said. "Did you like my voice? I told you we would tease him!"

"It was my sparrow bee that did it," Kuro boasted. He inspected the corpses. "I didn't know it was that poisonous! I hope they don't kill it. I want it back."

"What happens next?" Kiku asked.

"Now this fortress is mine and everyone in it must obey me," Shika said. "I have to take control, but first I must help Nagatomo."

"Oh," Kiku said, looking at Nagatomo for the first time. "Is he your friend? What a shame."

"Do you have any salve or medicine for this burn?"

"I only brought poisons," Kuro said. "I thought we came to kill, not to heal."

The fake wolf had wagged his tail at the sight of the boys and now he came closer to Nagatomo, who seemed mercifully to have lost consciousness, and sniffed at the ruined features, licking gently at the tears. Shika pushed him away, but Kiku said, "Let him lick it. Dogs and wolves clean with their tongue. Maybe Gen will help soothe the pain."

I cannot delay any longer, Shika thought. He ordered Gen to stay with Nagatomo and went to the door, signaling to the boys to follow.

"What can you hear, Kiku?"

"The men are in the inner yard. The one called Nobuto is trying to organize them to attack you. They sound reluctant."

"Where's my bee?" Kuro demanded.

"It's buzzing. I can hear it, but I'm not sure where."

"If they hurt it I'll kill them," Kuro muttered.

The doors had all been left open as the men fled through them. Sword in hand, Shika strode through the passages and out into the courtyard.

The milling, arguing warriors fell silent. One or two set arrows to their bows and trained them on him.

He said, "Kumayama no Jiro no Sademasa, brother of Shigetomo, uncle of Kazumaru, now known as Shikanoko, is dead. No man killed him. He was punished by Heaven for his faithlessness and cruelty. I have returned to take up my inheritance and challenge the tyrants in Miyako and Ryusonji. I will restore the rightful emperor to the throne. Those of you who loved my father and who will serve me, kneel and swear allegiance. Anyone who wants to oppose me can do it now, with the sword."

One by one the men put their weapons away and fell to their knees. Only Nobuto remained standing. He looked around and saw he was alone.

"You cowards!" he screamed. "You forget our lord so quickly? An imposter has scared you with his magic tricks and his accursed creatures. I will prove there is one man left in Kumayama."

He rushed at Shika with drawn sword and gave such a slashing blow it would have cut Shika in half had he remained where he was. He leaped sideways, evading the blade, and immediately found himself parrying a frenzied attack. He had killed the two men on the road from a distance, with arrows, and Gessho had already been weakened by poison when he had fought him with the sword. Now he faced a grown man in the prime of life and full strength, a warrior far more experienced than he was, made fearless by desperation.

None of the watching men made any attempt to help him and he realized he was being put to the test before them. If he won this combat, as a warrior not as a sorcerer, they would follow him unquestioningly.

He had no time for any more thoughts. He was fighting for his life.

Time halted. Everything else faded away. The only things that existed in the world were his opponent and the swords. He was no longer Shikanoko or Kazumaru or anyone. He was a being of pure instinct and inexhaustible energy, with only one desire—to live. His will flowed through every stroke and every step, unbreakable and irresistible. His opponent was older and stronger, a better fighter in every way, a man who would not give up, even when blood streamed from ten or more cuts. When Nobuto's right arm was made useless by a slash to the wrist, he switched to the left.

Shika was also bleeding, and beginning to tire. He hated Nobuto for not surrendering, wondering how long he himself could continue.

Nobuto stumbled as something buzzed past his ear, distracting him.

Shika thought, *I must kill him before the bee does. He must die by my hand.*

With his last reserves of energy and strength he thrust forward, a clumsy, brutal stroke that, for once, Nobuto did not foresee. In fact, he was moving toward the sword, and his own force thrust himself onto it, taking it deep into his throat and out through the back of his neck.

His eyes widened as blood gushed from his mouth. His legs gave way as the neck bones shattered. Hatred flashed briefly in his expression and then his soul fled his destroyed body.

The sparrow bee hurtled toward Shika, making him think he had won the fight only to die the same choking death as his uncle. He stood still, determined to show no fear. The sparrow bee buzzed briefly around his head and, when he did not move, swooped once more over the kneeling men and then flew beyond the palisade toward the forest.

After the bodies were burned and the ashes buried before the ground froze, Shika cleared the fortress of all traces of his uncle, adding his clothes and all his possessions to the fire. Once Nobuto was dead, the men were all ready to serve Shika, and within a few days he took half of them with him to Kuromori. They surprised the small besieging Miboshi force, killing them all. After relieving Kongyo and his men, Shika would have advanced on Matsutani, but the first snowfall of the year made him retreat to Kumayama for the winter.

As Kongyo had advised him, the snow would protect him, but, within the fortress, he had another problem, the women: Sademasa's wife, several concubines, and children. He did not know what to do with them.

"You should be ruthless," advised Kiku, who seemed to

have absorbed the essential elements of warrior culture in a few weeks. "They will only create more trouble for you later."

"Your uncle would have killed you," Kuro added.

"Yes!" Kiku exclaimed. "And look what happened because he did not. That proves my argument."

"They are my cousins," Shika said. "If I spare them and bring them up, they will be grateful and loyal."

"I would hate any man who spared my life," Kiku said.

"Me, too," Kuro agreed.

"But why? Wouldn't you be grateful?"

Kiku frowned. "I would feel in his power, as if I owed him something. I couldn't bear it."

"We could kill them," Kuro offered. "It would be good practice and I could try out some of the other insects."

The fortress was freezing, despite braziers placed here and there, and the boys' words and their calm faces made Shika feel even colder. He forbade them curtly to do any such thing, yet over the winter, one by one, the children died. Two suffered vomiting and diarrhea, one bled to death from mysterious puncture holes as if she had been attacked by leeches, one had convulsions, another croup. Of the women, two begged to be allowed to shave their heads and become nuns, one went mad after the death of her child and ran out into the forest. They found the body half-eaten by wolves in the spring. The others, including Sademasa's wife, took their own lives, like warrior women, with a knife in the throat.

From this Shika learned that the boys did not obey what

he said but followed what they perceived were his secret desires and were themselves unmoved by compassion or pity. He was torn between regret at the deaths and relief that the problem was solved in a way that gave him a reputation for ruthlessness.

9

HINA

Hina had been in Nishimi for four months. She was kept busy with the endless lessons that Takaakira had arranged for her: lute, poetry, classics, history, literature, genealogy. Mostly she enjoyed them, and she worked hard at her studies, practicing music daily and writing poems in reply to the ones Takaakira sent her. He returned hers with corrections and suggestions, which both annoyed and saddened her but also made her determined to write just one with which he could find no fault.

He supervised her progress, coming to her rooms every afternoon to listen to her sing and play. He did not praise her often, with the result that she remained unaware of her gifts and retained the unself-consciousness of a child.

Her teachers were the two elegant women who had come from Miyako, across Lake Kasumi. The younger one, Sadako, provided instruction in poetry and music, while

Masako, older and stricter, was an expert in classics and history and had a passion for genealogy. Both women brought their own servants. Bara looked after Hina, and there were also cooks and maids, grooms and gardeners, and various warriors, Takaakira's retainers, who had appropriated the long, low building to the left of the stables as their quarters. They challenged one another to horse races and archery competitions, went hunting in the forest and along the lakeshore, and kept themselves busy while waiting hopefully for orders to attack the Kakizuki forces, who had retreated to Rakuhara, several days' journey farther west.

The house was built in the style of a country palace, both rustic and luxurious. Its rooms stood around three sides of a square whose fourth side was open to the lake to capture cool breezes off the water in summer. On the west a bamboo grove, with a garden in front of it, shaded the residence from the setting sun. A stream had been diverted from the lake to flow through the garden. To the north was a stretch of pasture where many horses were kept; the stables stood on its edge, facing south to keep the horses warm in winter.

The lake itself protected the house from the dangerous northeast, and a shrine stood on the shore where, Hina had learned, the Lake Goddess was worshipped and honored with offerings of wine, fruit, and rice.

Mostly the shore was sandy, but the house was built on an elevated piece of land, where cliffs rose above the lake and the water below was deep. Wooden steps led down over the boulders to a jetty, where fishing vessels were tied up and trading boats came whenever the weather permitted.

Lady Masako told Hina that the beautiful house had belonged to a nobleman, Hidetake, who was a close friend of the former Crown Prince, and held a high position in the court when it was under Kakizuki sway. His wife, Masako told her, had been wet nurse and foster mother to the Prince's son, Yoshimori, who was now, some still dared think, though not say openly anywhere east of Rakuhara, the true emperor, if he was still alive.

Masako was careful to emphasize that this was an error, that the current emperor, the nephew of the Prince Abbot, was legitimate and blessed by Heaven, but her devotion to the truth would not allow her to omit the other line altogether.

Even in Nishimi, far removed from the capital, they could not escape the disasters that had afflicted the country since the death of the Crown Prince and the defeat of the Kakizuki. The estate had once been prosperous and had cultivated wet and dry fields of rice, millet, beans, and taro and hundreds of mulberry, apricot, persimmon, and mandarin trees. It had raised silkworms and woven silk, and had traded its own produce, and goods from the west, across the lake with the merchants of Miyako and Kitakami. Now it had fallen into disrepair, hit by the natural disasters and the defection of most of its stewards and managers. Takaakira spent the first months he was there trying to organize replacements, save what he could of the harvest, and prepare the house for winter.

One day, in the eleventh month, a messenger came by

horse from Miyako, wearing Lord Aritomo's crest on his surcoat.

"His Lordship will be returning to the capital, no doubt," Bara said as she combed Hina's hair in preparation for Takaakira's afternoon visit.

"Why? I thought we were staying here all winter," Hina said.

"Lord Aritomo isn't going to keep his most important retainer buried in the country forever, is he? But he won't take you with him. You will stay here, where you are safe."

"I wish I could go home, to my real home," Hina said wistfully.

"Don't fret, my chick—I mean, Lady Hina—you are luckier than most."

Bara often called her pet names and treated her like her younger sister, but not in the presence of the teachers or Takaakira.

When Takaakira came, he seemed preoccupied and reluctant to leave. Hina played for him, and sang an *imayo* that Sadako told her had been popular in the court a few years before. She read to him from a book of poems, but nothing penetrated his dark mood.

"Do you still have your Kudzu Vine Treasure Store?" he interrupted.

"Yes," she said. "I try to read a little every day. Shall I fetch it now?"

"No, I just wanted to know it was safe. And the box, do you still have that?"

"Yes," she said.

He nodded, without saying anything. Then he remarked, "It has been very cold today. It will be snowing in the mountains, and in my country, in the north. Bara must take great care of you, so you do not fall sick. No one must come in here unless they have been purified and prayed over."

"I wish you did not have to go away," Hina said.

"I wish it, too, my dear child. I don't want to leave you. I will find out what Lord Aritomo wants and return as soon as I can. But I am afraid it may not be before spring."

Hina missed him. The palace seemed empty without his presence and, though her lessons continued in the same manner, she was less inspired to study hard without his criticism and occasional admiration. Apart from music, which she truly loved—she would play the lute all day if she could—her attention wandered. She began to dwell on the past in a way she had not allowed herself until now. She recalled her life at Matsutani, the games with her little brother, Tsumaru, and Haru's children, Kaze and Chika. She missed the outdoor pastimes, the horses her father taught her to ride, the dogs that ran through the woods with them. She missed the Darkwood itself, its mysterious presence always around them. She began to sing the songs and ballads she had learned at Haru's knee after her mother died, and often she included the lament for the dragon's child, who in her mind had become one with Tsumaru.

It made her sad, reminding her of the night in the capital when Shikanoko had told her how Tsumaru had died, when she had waited in vain for her father to come home. Grief and her childish love for Shika were inextricably entwined in her heart.

Many of the songs were sad, set in the season of autumn, which suited her melancholy mood. Sometimes she pretended she was the Autumn Princess, which was what she had learned everyone called Lord Hidetake's daughter. She liked the name—it sounded sorrowful and beautiful at the same time. She had suspected for months that that was why Takaakira had been sent here. It suited him as a place to hide her, but all the time he was listening to her music and poems, supervising her lessons and the restoration of the estate, he had expected the Autumn Princess to turn up here at her old home.

"He waited for her all autumn," she said to herself. It suggested a poem and she let her mind play idly with the words, but really it would work only as a love poem, and she did not think Takaakira was waiting like a lover. Rather, he and Lord Aritomo had set an ambush, a trap from which the Princess would not escape alive.

Where was she now? Had they decided she was dead and so there was no need to wait for her anymore? And Shika-noko, had he also departed for that other world, like her father and her brother, her mother, everyone she had ever loved? These thoughts saddened and subdued her. Her teachers and Bara noticed her changed mood and thought she was pining for Takaakira. They suggested more outdoor activities, when the days were fine.

It continued to be very cold, with overcast skies. The

palace was constructed for the hot, humid weather of summer and the airy rooms were freezing. Sadako and Masako both caught colds and kept to their own quarters for several days. Hina's fingers were too numb to hold a pen or a plectrum; like her toes, they were chilblained and itched and ached. She and Bara slept under piles of quilted clothes, snuggling together to keep warm.

One morning, there was a sudden change in the weather. The wind blew from the south and the sun appeared, low in the sky, but warm. Hina woke early, and Bara, who was usually restless all night from the cold, was still deeply asleep. Hina was seized by the desire to go outside.

The pasture had been white with frost every morning for weeks, but this day it was bare and brown. The horses, with their shaggy winter coats, were grazing on the stalks of dried grass. Hina leaped down the cliff path—there was no one around to tell her to walk sedately. Some fishermen were already at the water's edge preparing boats and nets, taking advantage of the sudden warmth. She skirted them, not speaking to them. Farther along the shore, beyond the cliffs, a flock of plovers rose into the air at her approach, uttering plaintive cries.

A horse whickered in the distance and she turned in the direction of the sound. It neighed more loudly, then began to trot to her, slowly, clumsily because of its swollen belly. Behind it, cantering freely, was the silver white stallion.

"Risu!" Hina cried. "Nyorin!"

The mare reached her, almost knocking her over in her eagerness to nuzzle her. Hina held her head, stroking the broad forehead, then put her other hand on the belly and felt the foal kick. She was filled with an emotion so intense it brought tears to her eyes. Nyorin lowered his head and breathed in her face. She stroked his soft pink nose.

"Where is Shikanoko?" she said aloud, and then called, "Shikanoko!" Her voice sounded tiny, fainter than the plovers' cries.

The horses wore harnesses, and on Risu's back a bundle from which the neck of a lute emerged. Hina could not reach to touch it.

It was like a dream, filled with strange images that must have some significance but that she could not interpret. All she could think was that Shikanoko had fallen and was lying injured somewhere nearby, in the rice fields or on the lakeshore.

"Show me where he is," she said to the mare, and took the reins in her hand. She would have liked to ride, but she was afraid of hurting the unborn foal, and Nyorin was far too tall for her to mount without help.

Risu seemed to understand, for she began to walk purposefully along the shore toward the little shrine to the Lake Goddess. A vermilion bird-perch gate stood right in the water, and opposite it was a small hut. It was empty, occupied only at the seasonal festivals, and, though the farmers and fishermen left offerings at the outside altar, ringing the bell and making requests, no one ventured inside. The Lake Goddess was known to be unpredictable and capricious, and no one wanted to risk inadvertently offending her.

Hina looked around. There was no one in earshot. The

fishermen had launched their boats and were slowly rowing across the lake. She climbed the steps and listened at the door, then called quietly, "Is anyone there? Shikanoko?"

She heard the smallest of creaks from the floor within, as if someone were tiptoeing over it. Then a woman's voice replied, "Who are you? Why do you say that name?"

"Who are *you*?" Hina whispered. "And why do you have his horses?"

"You know them? Tell me their names."

"The mare is Risu and the stallion, Nyorin," Hina said. "Let me in, we cannot talk like this."

"I will let you come in, as long as you are alone. But be warned, I have a sword."

"I am alone," Hina said, and pushed open the door.

It was still dim inside the shrine. The room smelled of mildew and dust, and a faint scent of lamp oil, like a memory of summer nights. A young woman stood before her, the sword in her hand, on her back a small ceremonial bow. Her matted hair was tied in a horse's tail, held back from her face by a headband. She wore leggings under a short jacket, the clothes filthy, hardly better than rags. Her face was dark from dirt and weather.

They stared at each other for a few moments, then Hina said, "I am Kiyoyori's daughter. But can you be the Autumn Princess?"

"I used to be called Akihime." She lowered the sword and said formally, "Your father was a brave and loyal man. I am grateful for his sacrifice. He and my father died on the same day."

Hina felt one sob rise in her chest, but she fought it down. "No one knew for certain. Did you see him die?"

Akihime looked at her with pity. "No, but—well, I will tell you one day, but not now. Why are you here? How did you survive the massacre in the capital?"

"A warrior saved me. Yukikuni no Takaakira. He brought me here to hide me."

"For what purpose?"

After a pause, Hina said, "He wants to make me his wife. He is educating me to be a perfect woman, while the rest of the world forgets that Kiyoyori's daughter ever existed."

"But you are still a child," Akihime exclaimed.

"Not for much longer," Hina said.

"Let's hope the Miboshi are overthrown before that time! I did not know that Takaakira would be here. I came because my family owns this estate. I thought I could hide here."

"He has been waiting for you," Hina said. "They expected you to come. You are not safe here."

"I don't know where else to go," Akihime said. "I would have come before, or hidden somewhere else, but I had the horses. I could not abandon them. I've had to fight to hang on to them, so many people wanted to steal them from me. I have been traveling up and down the highways, but, even though I now look like this, people were beginning to talk about me. Men were seeking me out to challenge or capture me. My father taught me how to fight, but I did not expect to be defending myself against thieves and rogues on the road. I can't fight, or travel, much longer."

She opened her jacket and showed Hina the swell of her belly.

Hina felt her eyes narrow and a wave of jealousy and anger flooded through her. Barely controlling her emotions, she said, "Is that why you have Shikanoko's horses?"

"You are quick to guess! What a clever child you are. Yes, he is the father." Akihime's expression turned somber, but her voice suggested something else.

The last thing Hina wanted to be told was that she was a child. She lost all desire to help Akihime. She just wanted her to disappear, or be dead. But then she remembered that this young woman served the Emperor, for whom both their fathers had died. They were tied together by powerful bonds.

"Where is Shikanoko now?" she said.

"I don't know. The horses attacked him. He was unconscious when we left him."

I would never have left him! "Is he dead?"

"I don't know," Aki said again.

"You said *we*? Were you with the child Emperor?"

Aki nodded.

"And where is he now?" Hina said, looking around, as if Aki might have hidden him somewhere within the shrine.

"I will tell you the whole story, I promise you, but not at this time. I must decide what to do next."

"Takaakira is away," Hina said. "Some crisis arose that meant he had to go to the capital. I'm not sure when he will return. Most of the former servants ran away. I wonder if there are any left who would know you?"

"It is years since I have been here. I don't think they would recognize me."

"The men are on the lookout for you. But they are expecting a young princess, not . . ."

"A vagrant with child." Akihime smiled bitterly.

"Stay here if you are not afraid," Hina said.

"I have been afraid for months, but here I . . . I was going to say I wasn't afraid. I was dedicated to the Lake Goddess, who is a manifestation of All-Merciful Kannon, as a child. I used to hide here from my nurses and no one dared come to find me. I even ate the rice cakes and other offerings—the Goddess never punished me. But now she no longer protects me. I broke my vow of purity—I was supposed to be a shrine maiden at the Goddess's shrine at Rinrakuji. She is punishing me now."

She looked so sad Hina was moved to pity. "I'll look after you. I'll fetch some food and leave it here, and later I'll send Bara to bring you to the house."

"And what will the men say when they see two strange horses, with saddle and bridles?"

"I'll take them to the stables now and say I found them. It's not the first time stray horses have turned up." Hina could not help smiling. "And Risu will have her foal safely here. Do you think I'll be able to keep it as mine?"

"No one is more worthy of it," Aki said, smiling, too.

"I saw the lute," Hina said. "Do you play?"

"I try, but I cannot master it."

"May I play it?"

"I will tell you a secret," Aki said. "It is Genzo, the Emperor's lute. Take great care of it and keep it hidden."

Hina went outside cautiously. The horses waited close to the shrine. Hina stood on the steps to reach Risu's back, untied the bundle with the lute, and tucked it under one arm. Then she took Risu's reins in one hand and Nyorin's in the other, and began to lead them to the stables.

She had gone less than halfway when she saw Bara running across the pasture. The other horses tossed their heads and ran away from her, kicking out and bucking as if it were spring. Then they circled back to inspect the newcomers, sniffing the air and neighing loudly.

Bara cried out, "Lady Hina, what are you doing?"

"Look what I found," Hina shouted back. "Stray horses!"

"Be careful, they may be dangerous."

"No, they are gentle," Hina said, but when Bara came closer and tried to take Risu's reins, the mare laid back her ears and showed her teeth.

"Behave!" Hina said and smacked her lightly.

"I don't like horses," Bara confessed. "They are so heavy and clumsy, they put their feet everywhere without looking, and they seem to be moody."

"They don't like people who are afraid of them," Hina said, remembering what her father had told her. "It makes them nervous."

"But what are you doing out so early?" Bara asked. "I woke and you were not in the house. The lord will be so angry if he finds out. Anything might have happened to you."

"I couldn't go back to sleep, and it felt suddenly warm. I just wanted to be outside on my own." Hina felt some contrition at Bara's concern, but it also irritated her.

Bara looked at her. "Well, it seems to have done you some good. Your eyes are bright and your cheeks rosy. But Lord Takaakira does not want you to look like a farm girl. He likes you languid and pale, like a lily."

"I would rather be a rose, like you, Bara!"

Bara smiled. "Next time, wake me up and I'll come with you. Here. Give me that bundle before you drop it." She took it from under Hina's arm. "What's in it? Is it a lute?"

"Yes, it was on the horse's back. I'll try it out later," Hina said, and then, "You would do anything for me, wouldn't you, Bara?"

"I would, my chick, as long as it does not get me into trouble with the lord."

Hina smiled but did not reply. They were now on the lower track that led to the stables and two men came running down to meet them, exclaiming in surprise at the sight of the horses. One was a groom Hina particularly liked, though she could not say why, since she had hardly ever spoken to him. But he looked cheerful and open-hearted, and he treated the horses gently. Now she noticed for the first time that Bara liked him, too, and perhaps he liked her back, for they exchanged a swift, almost secret smile and Bara's cheeks flushed, much more than Hina's.

He took Risu's reins from Hina and the other man took the stallion's. A boy ran from the stables and chased the herd of horses, which had been following them, back to the pasture. They cantered away, a wave of brown, black, and gray. Nyorin pulled back as if he would gallop after them.

"Whoa!" the groom cried, and Hina said, "Stay, Nyorin."

"Where did these beauties come from?" the man holding Risu said.

"I found them in the pasture."

"The mare is in foal," the man observed. "Getting close, by the look of her."

"You must take care of them," Hina said. "They will be mine. What is your name?"

"Saburo, lady." He bobbed his head to her. "You called the stallion something?"

"Nyorin," she said, adding quickly, "It means Silver, so I think it suits him."

"And the mare?" Saburo said. "Are you going to give her a name, too?"

Hina pretended to think. "How about Risu?"

"Very well, lady. I'll clean them up and feed them."

"I will come and see them later," Hina said as she patted the horses goodbye. They turned their heads to watch her go and whickered after her.

Bara made Hina sit on the veranda while she fetched water to wash her feet. It was as good a place to talk as any.

"Bara, dear," she said quietly. "There is someone hiding in the shrine."

"So the horses did not turn up alone?"

"No, it is a young woman and she is going to have a baby. She has nowhere else to go."

Bara continued washing Hina's feet with even more vigor, splashing water unnecessarily.

"Is it the person the lord has been waiting for?"

"How do you know that?"

"People talk about it. They wonder why Lord Aritomo allowed Takaakira to be absent from the capital for so long. There are a few left here who served Lord Hidetake and still consider themselves Kakizuki. That groom, Saburo, for example." Saying his name made Bara smile.

"And you, Bara?"

"I am from Akashi, the free city. I am neither Miboshi nor Kakizuki. But Lord Takaakira employs me and trusts me. I can do nothing against his wishes."

"Well, it could hardly be her," Hina said. "She is not a princess, she is a vagrant."

She sat quite still while Bara dried her feet, afraid she had already betrayed Aki, wondering how she could warn her.

"If Lady Hina expressly commands me to do something, I cannot disobey her," Bara said very quietly.

"What should I command you?" Hina said.

"The men will almost certainly search for the owner of the horses," Bara said.

"I thought you could fetch her to the house after dark, but how can we stop them looking in the shrine and finding her?"

"Better to hide her in plain view. So that someone else finds her, who is not looking for her."

"The fishermen," Hina whispered. "If they found her in the water they would think the Lake Goddess had delivered her to them."

"A young pregnant woman who tried to drown herself but was saved by the Goddess," Bara said, thinking aloud.

"Let's take offerings to the shrine now, in thanks for the horses," Hina said. "We will tell her our plan."

"I've just got your feet clean," Bara complained.

"You can do them again afterward. Go quickly, bring rice cakes and whatever else we have."

While Bara hurried off to the kitchen, Hina turned her attention to the lute. She untied the bundle and took it out, surprised at how shabby and ordinary it looked. She plucked a string; it responded reluctantly. It needed tuning, but beyond that she felt some deep-grained obstinacy that resisted her fingers and her will.

She was about to lay it down and put her sandals on again when she thought of something else. She decided to take the eyes to the shrine, too, so they would protect Aki-hime. Carrying the lute, she went quickly to her room, where the box that held them was hidden beneath a silk cloth. She could hear her teachers coughing from their quarters. They still sounded very unwell; there would be no lessons today.

She took the box out and left the lute in its place, then raised the lid and prayed quickly, recalling how, when Takaakira had opened the box in the house in Miyako, she had seen him transfixed by the eyes, unable to move until she closed the lid. She had never dared ask him what had happened to him. When she opened the box it was to pray to Sesshin and to water the eyes with her tears. Once Sadako had come up behind her and looked over her shoulder, saying in her gentle voice, "What have you . . . ?" which was as far as she got. She stood without moving, staring at the eyes, and then tears began to slide from her own eyes and trickle down her cheeks.

"Ah, what a wasted life," she murmured. "Yes, I see myself, shriveled and old, with no man's love and no children."

Hina had closed the box quickly and had been especially diligent and affectionate to Sadako for the next few days. Though she cried over the eyes to cleanse them and keep them moist, sometimes telling herself she was an orphan, alone in the world, hidden by a man who would one day force her to marry him, unlikely ever to see again the boy she truly loved, they did not really show her the devastating insights that others seemed to see.

In truth, when she kept her thoughts firmly in the present, neither grieving for the past nor fearing the future, she was not unhappy. Learning was a joy, her teachers were kind to her, Bara loved her.

She heard Bara call her name, and she closed the box and went back to the veranda. The air was warming up now, and it felt pleasant to sit in the sunshine and let Bara rub her feet and then fasten her sandals.

Bara had placed a tray on the boards. It held two small rice cakes, a slightly shriveled mandarin, and a sprig of red-berried sacred bamboo. "I did not dare make it too lavish," she said. "I didn't want to make anyone suspicious."

As she lifted the tray and stood up, she remarked, "You have your precious box, I see."

"I am going to lend it to the Lake Goddess," Hina replied.

"What's inside, my chick?"

"Have you never looked in?" Hina returned, knowing Bara's inquisitive nature.

Bara went red. "I did take a peek once, but all I saw was myself, all my regrets from the past, the stupid things I'd done, the way I treated my mother. It upset me, I'm telling you. I'd never look again."

"They are a man's eyes. Perhaps he was a sorcerer, perhaps he was a saint. He was blinded, unjustly, by my stepmother. I am their guardian until I can return them to Matsutani."

Hina was silent as they walked back to the shrine, wondering if that day would ever come.

The warmer weather had brought everyone outside. Retainers were exercising horses in the pasture. Fishermen were in their boats offshore, their wives and children on the beach, their gossip and laughter loud in the clear air. The surface of the lake was as still and smooth as a mirror.

The presence of so many people made Hina very nervous. She was sure someone would find their behavior unusual and would come to investigate. At the steps of the shrine she put the box down, so she could clap her hands to awaken the Goddess and alert Akihime. Bara laid the offerings on the step and pulled at the bell rope. It clanged above Hina's head as she spoke softly to Aki in between her prayers.

Goddess of the Lake, protect your child. "Lady, when there is no one around, come out and throw yourself in the water." *She was dedicated to you as a child, act now to save her.* "Let the fishermen find you." *Hide her in your depths and let your waves bring her to shore.* "My maid, Bara, will make sure you are looked after. I am leaving something here to protect you, but do not look at it." *Goddess of the Lake, bless these eyes and enable them to see clearly.*

There was a large gap between the top step and the bottom of the door and Hina pushed the rice cakes and the mandarin through it. She heard the faintest whisper.

"Thank you. I will do as you say. I will leave my sword here, for the Goddess. Please look after it. I will keep my knife so I can kill myself if I am discovered."

"That is not going to happen," Hina said. She had complete confidence in the Goddess and in Sesshin's eyes.

10

AKI

After Kiyoyori's daughter and the woman left, Aki ate the rice cakes, though they barely satisfied her. The baby was growing large and she was always hungry. She was also terribly thirsty. The mandarin was dry inside. She chewed each segment and sucked the peel, but its bitterness made her mouth and tongue sore. Then the baby shifted position, stretching and kicking, giving her an urgent need to urinate. She squatted in a corner close to the door, hoping the Goddess would not be offended, praying no one would see the water drip through the floor. The stream seemed endless, its noise deafening.

She scattered the remains of the mandarin peel over it to mask the smell, took the sword, and placed it behind the small altar at the back of the hut. Then she sat, leaning against the wall, gathering her strength and courage for the next move. She could see the merit in Hina's plan, but she did not look forward to committing her life to the chill water of the lake and the mercy of fishermen.

She must have slept a little. She dreamed of Kai and Yoshi, the last time she had seen them, a few weeks ago. She had been riding along the lakeside road when she noticed the boats plying their way along the edge of Lake Kasumi, had followed them, and that night had watched the performers on the shore. Yoshi and the monkey boy whose name she did not know tumbled with a group of monkeys. The older men threw them through the air. And Kai sat on the side with the other musicians and beat her drum. Aki was happy, for Yoshi looked content and healthy, and he and Kai had found each other again. They would look after each other. She crept away back to where she had left the horses, put her arms round Risu's neck, and cried into her mane. She thought of going to join them, for hadn't Lady Fuji told her to come back if she didn't like life as a shrine maiden? But she was afraid of facing Fuji and the other women of the boats and did not want to be made to give up the horses. So she had ridden away, but in her dream she went down and called out to them. They both turned toward her and she saw their faces, and then she woke up. A strong wind was shaking the hut and it had grown much colder. She was shivering and her legs were cramping. She was about to stand up and move around when she heard men's voices. Her heart seemed to fill her throat and pound deafeningly in her ears.

This is the end, she thought, and felt the baby shudder

inside her. "I'm sorry, I'm sorry," she whispered to it and grasped the knife.

Footsteps came closer, two or three men, on the steps.

"Could someone be hiding in the shrine?"

"It's possible, better check to make sure."

"What's in that box?"

"Are those . . . eyes?"

Aki hardly dared breathe. For a few moments no sound came from outside. Then inexplicably she heard sobbing, accompanied by broken phrases filled with regret and grief.

"Those men I killed treacherously."

"Those infants we slaughtered in Miyako!"

"I used to serve the Kakizuki. I betrayed them!"

"My favorite child—dead at six years old."

"Those girls we raped, how they screamed."

The wind howled more loudly and sleet pattered on the roof.

"Have we angered the Goddess?" she heard one man ask, and another replied, "Let's get out of here."

"Look at the lake!" cried the third. "A blizzard is coming!"

Their feet pounded down the steps and then Aki could hear nothing but the wind. She waited for a while, trying to control her breath, then opened the door a tiny crack. The wind forced it open further and snow flurried in, melting on the floor. She caught some flakes on her hand and licked them. The lake and the shore had disappeared; everything was turning white.

On the steps lay Hina's box. She forgot she had been warned not to look in it and her gaze fell on the eyes.

All the sorrows and regrets of the past year rose within her. If only she had not yielded to Shikanoko. If only she had not hidden from him afterward. She relived again the shock of seeing him broken on the ground. Why had she run away from him? She would never see him again and the baby would grow up fatherless. She had abandoned the Emperor, when she should be with him, protecting him with her life.

Her tears fell mingling with the snow. Her despair was complete. It was not to save her life that she ran into the lake. It was to drown herself.

11

MASACHIKA

Masachika knelt before Keita, the Kakizuki lord. It was months since he had arrived, on the orders of Takaakira, in Rakuhara, where the remains of the Kakizuki army had fled after the battles of Shimaura and the Sagigawa, when they had lost Miyako. He had been welcomed as Kiyoyori's brother, and indeed heir, for he was now legally the Kuromori lord, though no one actually called him that. In his usual way he had made himself useful, offered to carry out tasks no one else wanted to do, listened sympathetically to the endless recountings of battles lost, and even wrote many of them down, recording all the blame-erasing excuses of betrayal and injustice with murmurs of outrage. No one suspected him of being a spy, and, in truth, he had done little spying worthy of the name, though he now had a very clear idea of the strength and state of mind of the Kakizuki leaders. An unusually severe winter, with two months of gales and heavy snow, kept him, along with the rest of the Kakizuki, shivering in Rakuhara, where the cold winds penetrated every corner of the inadequate buildings and snow drifted up to the eaves.

He had plenty of time to compare the two lords, Keita and Aritomo, and concluded that on the whole he was lucky to have spent the winter in Rakuhara rather than Miyako. For, even in exile, Keita had not given up his love of luxury, his fondness for music, dancing, and poetry. The roof might leak, the ill-fitting shutters rattle, the chinks in the wall let in icy blasts, but Keita still slept under silk, ate from celadon bowls, and was entertained by his many court ladies and concubines. Aritomo possessed the capital and occupied two thirds of the Eight Islands, yet he chose to live frugally and despised ostentation. The craftsmen of Miyako were plunged into gloom and longed for the spendthrift Kakizuki to return so their businesses might prosper again. The craftsmen in the towns around Rakuhara rejoiced in the lively trade in ceramics, weaving, lacquerware, paper, and musical instruments.

Next to him, one of the elders, Yasutsugu, who had been a friend of his father's, said quietly, "A spy has come from Nishimi. We think the Autumn Princess is there. Only she knows what became of Yoshimori. It has filled everyone with hope. They are bringing the man here now so we can all hear what he has to say."

"What wonderful news," Masachika murmured.

A young man, in the clothes of a groom, was escorted in and prostrated himself before the gathering. When he sat up, Masachika could see he had the honest, open face that elicited trust, so useful for a spy. He told them a girl had been pulled from the lake by fishermen as the first snowstorm of the winter swept over Nishimi. She was pregnant and everyone assumed she was some vagrant who had tried to end her life. Her survival was considered something of a miracle and she was given shelter, though at first no one thought she would live. The icy water brought on a severe chill, followed by a fever, almost too fierce for her weakened frame to bear. But she survived and gave birth to a boy, who was thriving.

"How can the Autumn Princess be a mother, and abandoned?" Keita said doubtfully. "What was she doing alone? Who is the father of the child?"

It was so far from any noble person's experience it seemed unthinkable.

"Is she an imposter, hoping to gain some advantage?" Yasutsugu said.

The groom answered, "She herself has claimed nothing. She hardly speaks. I know this from Lady Hina, by way of my informant, Lady Hina's maid."

"Who is she, this Lady Hina?" Lord Keita was frowning slightly.

"Some young girl whom Yukikuni no Takaakira brought to Nishimi and is keeping there, without Aritomo's knowledge. The maid, Bara, showed me a knife that the pregnant woman had on her, and I recognized it as belonging to Lord Hidetake, whom I served in Miyako and Nishimi. I realized the woman must be his daughter, and the maid confirmed it."

"If she is truly the Autumn Princess we must bring her here and speak with her. But do we need to concern ourselves with Takaakira's plaything?"

Masachika tried to mask his intense interest. Hina had been the pet name for Kiyoyori's daughter. What if the child had been too young, too innocent to realize she should change it? He had thought Takaakira had been lying. Now he knew for certain he had been, and why.

"She is more than that," the groom said. "Inexplicable things have happened. The day Akihime was found, two strange horses turned up. They had harness that had once been of high quality. One, a mare, was pregnant, and gave birth to a foal the same day the child was born. The other is a stallion, fine-looking but strong-willed and stubborn. When they arrived Lady Hina gave them names, but they already answered to those names as if they had been called them before, for a long time, and I would swear they knew her. Horses cannot lie! Later, Bara told me the lady retrieved a magnificent sword that had been left in the shrine. She also took back to her room a box containing eyes."

"Eyes?" Lord Keita repeated.

"Eyes that make you look into your heart and see everything you ever lost, all your failures and regrets, all your hidden secrets. Those eyes apparently kept Takaakira's warriors from searching the shrine, where the Princess was hiding. They would have found her if they had gone inside. And then the Lake Goddess sent a storm, at Lady Hina's request."

Masachika knew it was his brother's daughter. Takaakira had told him she was dead so he could keep her for himself. His heart swelled with joy at this knowledge, which gave him power over the man who had humiliated him. Takaakira's contempt had stayed with him for months, fueling the jealousy and resentment he held for Aritomo's favorite. And all the time Takaakira had been deceiving his lord. *This will bring him down. I'll make sure of it.* He had to go to Nishimi himself, at once.

"So," the groom concluded, "Lady Hina is much more than a young girl who has caught the eye of Takaakira. I believe she is a warrior's daughter, but, even more than that, she is a sorceress in the making."

Lord Keita looked troubled. "We will consult the genealogies to find out who she is."

Masachika cleared his throat and said, "May I speak, lord?"

When permission was granted he went on. "Kiyoyori's daughter was known within the family as Hina. Perhaps this is her." He addressed the groom, "I am his brother, her uncle. I thought my beloved niece was dead." He allowed his voice to choke and raised his sleeve to his eye, as if to wipe away tears.

"I am happy to be the source of such good news," the man exclaimed, and directed a cheerful smile at Masachika, which he immediately suspected was false. His fears that he might be unmasked, never far from the surface, now rose to disturb him. Did the man know something about him? What did the smile really mean?

"What is your name?" he said.

"Saburo, lord," the man replied.

"You should return to Nishimi as soon as possible. What reason did you give for leaving?"

"My father's funeral."

"Very sad. And how did you get through the barrier?"

"I came over the mountains. There are many secret paths."

"You can show me," Masachika said. "We will return to Nishimi together and I will verify the truth of your report. If my lords agree," he added hastily, looking around at the elders and Lord Keita.

"Should we not rather prepare to attack Nishimi and rescue both the girls, before they are discovered?" Yasutsugu suggested.

"Takaakira has many men there," Saburo said. "Such an attack would only reveal the importance of the girls and put their lives in danger. Better to try to spirit them away. I can bring them here."

"If she truly is the Autumn Princess and if I recognize Hina as my niece, we will do that together," Masachika said.

Saburo could not hide his reluctance. "It is a hard journey over the mountains, and how will I explain who you are at Nishimi?"

"I have had worse journeys," Masachika replied. "I will dress as a groom, pass as a relative of yours, seeking work."

"I mean no offense, lord, but you do not speak like any relative of mine."

"You think I can't mimic you?" Masachika said in a

familiar way, immediately regretting it, as the elders all stared at him in astonishment.

"You are a man of hidden talents," Yasutsugu remarked.

"All in the service of Lord Keita and the Kakizuki," Masachika said hastily.

"Do you swear it?"

"On my brother's soul," he said and prostrated himself before them.

Clothes were brought for Masachika and some food prepared for traveling. As soon as it was ready and he had changed, they set out.

Saburo looked him over critically as they walked through the north gate of Rakuhara, past the guards, who wished Saburo a safe journey and screwed up their faces at Masachika, not recognizing him.

"Your hands give you away," Saburo said. "How long is it since they have held reins?"

"I have not ridden all winter," Masachika replied. He thought he heard contempt in the groom's voice and decided he would kill him before they came to Nishimi. However, he knelt and rubbed his hands in the spring mud on the path. Small yellow flowers bloomed along its edge, attracting early bees. The sun was warm, but there was still a trace of winter in the air and snow lingered on the slopes of the mountains they had to cross. It was a little after noon. Night still fell early; they had less than half a day of walking ahead, unless Saburo intended to walk all night. Masachika tried to recall what phase the moon would be in. Surely it was coming up to full, so there would be plenty of light. If he'd known he was going to make this sudden trip, he would not have stayed up so late the night before, nor would he have drunk quite so much. His head ached already.

Saburo set a fast pace, even after the slope steepened and the climb began. The path gradually became more overgrown until it was scarcely more than a fox track and they often had to go on hands and knees to crawl through the undergrowth. After they passed a den, where they could hear newborn cubs mewing and could smell the rank fox odor, the path disappeared completely. Saburo seemed to be following some course he had marked on his descent, carefully placed stones, bent twigs, marks scratched on rocks. Masachika tried to pick them out and realized he could not. Without Saburo, he would be lost. Reluctantly, he decided to let him live until they arrived at Nishimi. He spent the rest of the day devising his punishment and death.

When it was too dark to walk farther, Saburo stopped by a rocky outcrop. The ground next to it was flat, sandy rather than stony, and the rocks offered a little shelter.

"We will rest here until moonrise. Sleep if you can. I'll keep watch."

Masachika sat down, trying to hide the fact that his limbs were trembling from the climb. He had no appetite, but he forced himself to swallow the rice ball Saburo held out to him. It was flavored with dried shrimp and salted plum and increased his intense thirst. Snowmelt had gathered in small hollows in the rocks, and they drank from that, licking the last moisture with their tongues.

He did not want to sleep, too aware that while he needed Saburo to guide him, the groom did not need him. If the man suspected him, as he was sure he did, he could easily dispatch Masachika in the mountains and no one would ever know. Masachika was determined to live, for if he could deliver both the Autumn Princess and Kiyoyori's daughter to Miyako, he would win the most profound gratitude from Lord Aritomo and avenge himself on Takaakira.

However, when he lay down exhaustion overtook him, and dreams began to appear behind his eyelids. He slept without meaning to. He heard familiar voices speaking to him: his father, Tama. He could not catch what they were saying, but it seemed important. Then, suddenly, a dark brown foal stood before him. *It looks like Kiyoyori*, he thought in surprise. *How can a horse so resemble my brother?*

He woke, his heart pounding. He sat up swiftly and looked around. The moon had cleared the mountain peaks and lit up the rocks around him. He was alone.

He leaped to his feet, cursing aloud, but then he heard a rustle from the bushes and Saburo appeared.

"What's the matter?" said the groom. "I just went for a piss. Did you think I'd abandoned you?" He was regarding Masachika with unpleasant shrewdness.

"You are a Kakizuki lord," Saburo went on, "brother to the great Kiyoyori. I have been entrusted with the task of getting you to Nishimi and helping you rescue the Princess and your niece. I know nothing about you, except what the mountain forces you to reveal of yourself. But, already, you have shown you do not trust me. Only the untrustworthy find it impossible to trust others."

Masachika did not reply. He relieved himself behind the rocks, then followed Saburo as they began to climb upward, under the third-month moon.

12

HINA

Throughout the long, cold winter, Hina had worked at mastering the lute. She had never known an instrument like it. Many times she felt like consigning it to the fire. She would gladly watch it burn, for all the pain it had caused her. It went out of tune, its strings snapped for no reason or seemed to turn sticky under the plectrum so it slipped from her fingers. Even Sadako could not persuade it to play. Yet every now and then it relented and a burst of music would come from it, filled with such purity and yearning it brought tears to her eyes.

At those times she wanted to take it to Aki, but it seemed wiser not to spend too much time with her. The girl lived in the servants' quarters and Hina saw her only once or twice, when she pretended to be more of a child than she really was and went with Bara to the kitchen to be given precious treats, dried persimmons, pickled plums, red bean paste, which grew more scarce as winter dragged on.

When she recovered from her fever, Aki worked in the kitchen, after a fashion, for it was obvious she had neither training nor natural skill, but, as her time drew nearer, it was considered unsafe for her to be there, both for her sake and that of the household, for if childbirth were to take place suddenly in the kitchen, the residence would become polluted. She was confined, with another woman who was expecting a child, to a small detached hut. It was dark and cold, and Hina, who saw it once, thought it a most inauspicious place to give birth.

Aki's labor was long and agonizing and no one expected her to survive it. Risu went into labor on the same day. It was also long and difficult—the groom, Saburo, had to pull the foal from her body—but the mare recovered quickly from the delivery, with Saburo's help, and nursed her foal immediately.

Hina had not known it was possible to adore a horse so much. From the moment she set eyes on the foal, the morning after his birth, when he was already standing on wobbly legs beside Risu, she had been in love with him. She had to see him several times a day, and she lay awake at night longing for morning so she could feast her eyes on him again. She made garlands of spring flowers and hung them around his neck, brushed his coat, and polished his little hooves. His mother was brown and his father, Nyorin, almost white, but the foal's coat was as dark as coal, so she called him Tan.

"He will turn gray, or silver like his father, after his first year," Saburo said. "All grays are born brown or black. He is going to be a fine horse. And see how he loves you, Lady Hina."

Whenever she went to the pasture the foal ran to greet her and followed her closely, breathing at her neck. Sometimes he fixed his huge dark eyes on her as though he would speak at any moment.

"What is it, my darling Tan?" she crooned to him, bringing her face close to his, and felt she was on the point of understanding him.

She loved the baby, who had been born on the same day, almost as much. Both had been difficult births for different reasons. The mare was so old, the girl so young. Aki was very ill after the delivery and could not feed him; the other woman luckily was able to nurse him along with her own baby girl. Aki whispered that his name was to be Takeyoshi, and for now they called him Takemaru: little bamboo shoot, little warrior, for *take* could mean both. He had a shock of black hair and a face that seemed old and wise. He was active and did not sleep much. His foster mother's young sister sometimes carried him around on her back, but mostly Bara looked after him. Often she walked with Hina to show the baby to the horses.

"This is your twin, Take," Hina would say, taking the baby from Bara and showing him to the foal. "He will be your horse, for you were born on the same day at the same hour."

Yet, even as she spoke, she felt all the uncertainty of the

future. They would not be able to conceal Aki and the baby forever. Snow still lay on the slopes and the nights were very cold, but one day the wind turned and blew from the east. Spring had come, and surely Takaakira would return soon.

The next day, Saburo was not at the stables. Bara told Hina his father had died and he had gone back to his village for the funeral. His absence added to Hina's unease. She realized she had come to depend on him and to trust him. Bara also was on edge and anxious.

The wind blew more and more strongly and spring came in a rush, leaves appearing on the trees, birds calling in the early morning. One day, Hina went with Bara and the baby to the pasture. She was carrying the lute, for she had dreamed in the night that she had offered it to the Lake Goddess and it had begun to play on its own. It had looked different in the dream, no longer shabby and battered but gleaming rosewood, inlaid with gold and mother-of-pearl. She could still hear its exquisite music in her head. She also brought Sesshin's book, the Kudzu Vine Treasure Store, intending to read a little in the quiet of the shrine while Bara entertained the baby.

As usual Tan cantered up to her, nuzzling her and breathing in her breath, wrinkling his lips and snorting over Take, who laughed and wriggled with delight.

"Look," Bara said, pointing out over the lake. "A boat is coming!"

Hina's heart plunged to her belly. "Is it Lord Takaakira?"

"It could be."

They stared out over the water, dazzled by the sun, the wind bringing tears to their eyes. From the boat came strands of music and laughter, and a strange high sound, like an animal squealing.

"That doesn't sound like the lord," Bara said, and they both gave a gasp of relief at the same time. Bara looked guilty as she smiled. "It must be one of the market boats. They have been driven across the lake by the wind. I suppose they were trying to get to the Rainbow Bridge, and Majima."

"What beautiful names," Hina said. "Where are they?"

"On the other side of the lake. They will be holding the twenty-fifth-day market there today. I think they might be performers, for those cries are monkeys."

"Monkeys!" Hina exclaimed. "Let's go down to the dock and see them. Little Take would like that, wouldn't you?"

The foal gave a strange sound, startling them. He was gazing intently toward the stables. His body trembled all over.

"Oh, it's Saburo," Bara said. "Did Tan recognize him?" She waved, holding the baby in one arm.

Saburo and another man were walking past the barracks, where the warriors were preparing for another day, getting out their bows to practice archery, repairing and polishing armor.

"Who's that with him?" Hina said.

"I don't know," Bara said, sounding puzzled. "Another groom, perhaps? I haven't seen him around here before."

Hina was watching the way Saburo walked, noncha-

lant but wary, eyes flicking around as if searching. He saw
Bara and made a slight gesture with his head. *What does it
mean?* Hina wondered. She would never know. Suddenly
Saburo was not walking anymore. The man alongside him
grabbed him and twisted him into a strange position, one
arm behind his back. The knife at his throat. Shouts of
surprise. The men on their feet, swords drawn. Saburo on
his knees. The sudden gush of blood. Bara's scream. The
foal pushing her, pushing her to the shore.

*Run, daughter. It is your uncle. He will hand you over to
the Miboshi.*

"Akihime!" she cried. "Bara, we must warn Akihime."
Then she stopped, terrified the murderer had heard her.

Bara stood whimpering as if in shock. Hina held the
lute and the text in one hand and with the other seized the
baby from her. She looked around, frantic. Where should
she run to?

The boat had reached the shore. The easterly wind had
dropped. She could hear laughter, the careless laughter
of ordinary people. She thought of what she was leaving
behind. Takaakira, her life of music and learning. The eyes?
How could she leave the eyes? They were in her room. And
the sword? Akihime's sword, which she had returned to
the shrine as an offering to the Lake Goddess.

Bara was stumbling, like a sleepwalker, toward Saburo's
fallen body. The other man, Hina's uncle, was gesticulat-
ing, explaining to the men who surrounded him. Hina
heard their cries of amazement and triumph. Akihime was
betrayed.

She felt the lute pull her. She ran to the dock, Take

bumping and chuckling in one arm, the lute and the scroll in the other. The lute was changing before her eyes just like in her dream. It became beautiful, gleaming in the morning sun, and as she approached the boat it began to play, the glorious music echoing through the sudden calm.

Then with a rush the wind rose again.

"Ah, here comes the westerly!" called the helmsman. "We will get to the market, after all!"

"Take me with you!" Hina cried, as the oarsmen turned the boat and the west wind filled the sail. The lute was almost deafening her. Behind her Tan was neighing.

Two boys, a few years younger than she was, stood on the deck, surrounded by monkeys.

"What are you doing with that lute?" one of them shouted to her, as the boat skimmed the side of the dock.

"Take it!" Hina put Take down for a moment and threw the lute to them and then the text. Then she picked Take up and holding him tightly in her arms jumped after them. But the boat had already veered around and the baby hampered her. She fell into the deep water next to the dock. She did not dare release her grip on Take. He struggled and screamed, choking on the icy water. The beautiful robes Takaakira had given her were now deadly, filling with water, as heavy as iron.

13

MASACHIKA

The following day Masachika took Akihime to Miyako, crossing the lake by boat, using the same westerly wind. He did not go to Aomizu but went directly to Kasumiguchi. He was troubled that Hina and the baby had disappeared, apparently drowned in the lake, though there was no trace of their bodies—it would have been tidier to scoop all three up in the one net—but he had the main catch secure in his hands. The weather was worsening and he did not want to get caught on the open lake in a storm.

He searched the house and the shrine before leaving and found enough evidence to prove that Takaakira had been keeping the young girl in the house for nearly a year. When he questioned the two women, who were teachers of some kind, they swore they had not known who their pupil was, but attested to her intelligence, gentle nature, and talent for music and poetry, none of which interested Masachika in the slightest. But in her room he found the box and that interested him greatly.

He remembered what the groom had said but could not resist the temptation to look inside. Immediately sadness swept over him. He felt anew the loss of Tama and Matsutani. He saw himself always, all his life, compared with Kiyoyori, and falling short. He saw his self-serving nature, his jealousy, his treachery. Bitter regrets assailed him for all that might have been. While his mind was so open and vulnerable, one of his flashes of insight came to him. The eyes were Sesshin's and would give him mastery over the spirits at Matsutani. He closed the box, and made sure it traveled with him.

He came upon the sword in the shrine. It had been placed behind the altar, and he marveled that no one had stolen it, for he had never seen a finer blade. He felt an unusual reluctance to touch it, and when he lifted it the sword felt heavy and unwieldy, but after a few moments it settled into his hand, and he was aware it had acquiesced in some way. It thrilled him, giving him hope that his life was about to turn around, that he would be well rewarded, that he would become a better man as a result. To his surprise, a prayer formed on his lips. He also found a ceremonial bow made of catalpa wood, but it made him feel uneasy and he decided to send it to Ryusonji. He was holding it in one hand and the sword in the other when he came out of the shrine. The horses were standing out in front, as if they had been waiting for him. They stared at him fixedly, and a shaft of terror pierced him as he recognized the foal from his dream.

Masachika did not dare voice his fears. He gave orders that the horses should be brought to Miyako, resolving to present them to the Prince Abbot. If the foal were possessed, the Prince Abbot would recognize the spirit.

The maid, Bara, was hysterical at the loss of her lover, which Masachika realized Saburo must have been, and useless, so he took the younger of the teachers, Sadako, with them, to wait on Akihime, for even though she was a fugitive she was still a nobleman's daughter. Akihime refused to speak and did not respond to any of his questions regarding Yoshimori, or the child to whom she had recently given birth, although when his patience gave out and he told her the boy had drowned, she wept silently.

Lord Aritomo inspected Aki as if she were a piece of art. Takaakira was in the room with them, but so far he had not spoken. Masachika glanced at him from time to time, trying to assess his reactions, but the lord of the Snow Country remained impassive.

The rain was teeming down. As Masachika had feared, the westerly had increased to a gale. Rivers were breaking their banks, destroying the spring plantings of rice and vegetables.

"You see," Lord Aritomo said, "I was right. She went to her childhood home. We only had to wait for her." He smiled tight-lipped, then addressed Masachika.

"Well done. You will be rewarded."

Masachika bowed. He had related how the groom Saburo had come to Rakuhara, but so far he made no mention of

Hina or the baby, nor did he say anything about the eyes or disclose the sword.

"Why are her arms bruised?" Aritomo said.

"She was about to cut her throat. I had to prevent her. She struggled against me."

Aritomo nodded.

"May I present the knife to you?" Masachika said.

Aritomo took it and inspected it carefully. "It is very fine. In a way I am sorry it does not come fresh with the blood of a princess, but, of course, she will be more use to us alive."

He turned to Takaakira, showing him the knife. "You would have had the honor of finding her, and earlier, if I had not summoned you back here to advise me on this upstart at Kumayama. What does he call himself?"

"Shikanoko," Takaakira replied.

"Tell Masachika about him."

"He is causing us some trouble by establishing a garrison between the capital and Minatogura. He attacked his family fortress at Kumayama and killed his uncle, who had become one of our vassals. Then he took over Kuromori at the beginning of the winter. Next will be Matsutani."

"What possible claim can he have to Matsutani?" Masachika exclaimed.

"Right of conquest, it is called," Aritomo said drily. "Don't be too concerned. He won't be there for long. We are going to use the Autumn Princess to draw him out. According to the Prince Abbot at Ryusonji he has strong feelings for her. Isn't that right, Princess?"

Akihime did not raise her head.

"He will try to rescue you, but he will die in the attempt," Aritomo said pleasantly. "But first you will tell us where to find Yoshimori, the false emperor."

"I don't know where he is," Akihime replied. "He was kidnapped from me. I have not seen him for months. But, as you well know, he is the true emperor. Isn't Heaven itself telling you that? If he is restored to the throne, these disasters will end."

The rain fell more heavily, as if the river itself had been drawn up from its bed and was emptying itself out over the city.

"Neither Shikanoko nor anyone else will be moving if this continues," Takaakira said. "All the rivers between here and Minatogura are in flood and the country is devastated."

"It is your evil doing that has caused it," Aki said. "You know how to bring back harmony between Heaven and earth."

"Silence!" Aritomo had gone pale and a muscle was twitching in his cheek. "Takaakira," he said in a tight voice. "Take the Princess away to Ryusonji. We will see what the Prince Abbot can find out from her. And have Masachika make a full report on the situation at Rakuhara."

The guards escorted Akihime out of the room. Takaakira and Masachika bowed deeply to Lord Aritomo and left together. Masachika followed the other man to a small room overlooking the garden. He was slightly worried that Takaakira would comment on the sword, but it was disguised in his old scabbard, and, in some way, he knew it was not going to draw attention to itself. The eyes were in their carved rosewood box, tucked inside the breast of his hunting robe. He wondered how much Takaakira knew about them.

A solid curtain of rain fell from the eaves and the once-beautiful garden was sodden. Water lay on the paths in huge puddles and all the pools were overflowing.

Masachika reported all he had learned during his months with the Kakizuki army—weapons, numbers of men and horses, fighting spirit—and described the luxury in which Lord Keita lived and, finally, Keita's hopes of finding Yoshimori.

Takaakira listened without comment, saying at the end, "Well, write it all down and bring the document to me at my house tomorrow. You can write, I suppose?"

Masachika noted the contemptuous tone and said blandly, "Of course," while thinking, *Don't be too quick to antagonize me, noble lord. You will be begging me, before too long. And don't forget that what you call your house is as much mine as yours.*

After Takaakira left, Masachika called for writing materials and something to eat and drink. All were supplied swiftly and politely. His status had risen, he concluded with considerable gratification. It took him some time to compose his report—his writing was adequate for recording the various exploits of warriors on the battlefield and he was familiar with that vocabulary, but, in striving to make his work both clear and elegant, he realized there were many words he was not sure of. He had to spell them out, rather than using their ideograms, and he feared it made the report look womanly, childish.

By the time he had finished, it was almost dark; the rain was heavier than ever. A servant came to remove the utensils, and he said he would spend the night where he was.

"Certainly, lord," she said, prostrating herself. "I will fetch some bedding."

When she returned, she brought new robes. "From Lord Aritomo," she murmured.

Masachika settled down for the night, under the padded silk, feeling reasonably pleased with himself.

The next day he presented himself at the house that had been his father's, and then Kiyoyori's, and was now occupied by Takaakira. He wore the new clothes, a brocade hunting robe and embroidered trousers. Together with the eyes in their box and the sword at his side, they gave him confidence, but even more than these, it was the secret he held in his heart that would put him on an equal footing with Takaakira.

The lord of the Snow Country looked as if he had spent a sleepless night. Masachika wondered, as he had several times already, what the man's purpose was in keeping Kiyoyori's daughter alive, in defiance of Aritomo's orders. Perhaps he had fallen in love with her—some men did lust after young girls—but why take such a risk? There were plenty of maidens in the city. Why choose Kiyoyori's daughter?

No doubt you are regretting your rashness now, he thought, raising his eyes insolently to Takaakira's pale face and hollow eyes.

He had presented the report and it lay on the floor at Takaakira's side. They were alone in the room and the rain was so loud, there was little chance of being overheard. Nevertheless Takaakira gestured that Masachika should move closer and whispered, "Did you find anyone else at Nishimi?"

Masachika pretended to look puzzled. "Lord?"

"A young girl was living there, my ward."

"Your ward?"

"Yes. She is called Hina."

"My niece, Hina? My brother's daughter?"

Takaakira did not say anything, but the expression on his face nearly compensated Masachika for all the petty humiliations he had endured. Nearly but not quite.

"She was believed to be dead," he said. "Can it be that she lives, after all? What joy!"

"What a scoundrel you are," Takaakira said. "How could you and Kiyoyori be brothers?"

"I'm surprised you are so free with your insults! I only have to mention my niece, and her lucky escape, to Aritomo and your life will be over."

"My life is over if she is dead," Takaakira said, somber.

Masachika stared at him. "It's true, isn't it, that no man

is without at least one weakness? A little girl has aroused your lust and you will throw everything away for that?"

"It's nothing like that. If I love her, it is as a daughter. She is a miracle, so intelligent, so gifted—but I will not discuss her with you."

"Well, many men sleep with their daughters," Masachika said crudely. "You would not be the first."

"Is she alive?"

"She ran away."

"Where to? Did anyone see her go?"

"I'm afraid I only have conflicting reports. One person said Hina jumped aboard a boat with the baby."

"What baby?"

"Akihime's son," Masachika said.

"You did not mention that earlier in the report," Takaakira said.

"I thought that information should rest between us for the time being. It may not matter, at all, for the other eyewitness said Hina fell into the lake with the baby in her arms. The water is very deep by the dock, and I believe they both drowned."

Takaakira covered his eyes with one hand. When he could speak he said, "I presume you searched the house and questioned the servants?"

"Of course," Masachika replied.

"Did you find a box containing . . . something unusual? A small, beautifully carved box of rosewood?"

"No, lord," Masachika said, feeling the box burn against his ribs.

"Then she must have taken it with her." The idea seemed to console Takaakira somewhat. "I cannot believe she is dead."

"Shall I make a more detailed report for Lord Aritomo?" Masachika managed to convey sympathy and menace at the same time.

Takaakira gave him a long, unwavering look of pure contempt. "I suppose we must come to some arrangement," he said. "If she is dead you can tell him what you choose. I will offer him my life in atonement. But if there is a chance she is alive, I must live and I must find her. What must I do to persuade you to keep this to yourself for now?"

"Are you suggesting I have a price?" Masachika said, pretending affront.

"We all have our price," Takaakira replied bitterly. "I just hope yours is not too high."

After this, Masachika found it easy to obtain permission from Takaakira to do whatever he desired. He rationed his requests, not wanting to push the lord too far. At one time he thought he would demand Kiyoyori's old house for himself, but decided against it. First he would secure Matsutani. Now that he had Sesshin's eyes, he was sure he could pacify and control the rebellious spirits. He proposed he should be the one to find Shikanoko and tell him they held the Autumn Princess in Miyako.

Takaakira agreed to approach Lord Aritomo, who gave his permission readily. It had been necessary to apply pressure to the Princess, enough to persuade her to talk but not so much as to kill her. Aritomo wanted her alive. She was watched day and night lest she try to take her own life, but despite the pain and the lack of sleep she revealed nothing other than that Yoshimori had been stolen away from her. She would not say where or how.

"If we bring them together," Aritomo said, "we will easily persuade the Princess to talk, and we will prevent any further Kakizuki uprisings.

"Secure Matsutani, send a message from there, and let me know Shikanoko's response immediately. Don't try to capture him or engage him in battle. The Prince Abbot wants him to be drawn into the capital so he can be taken alive."

Once again Masachika found himself at the head of a band of men riding toward Matsutani. The Prince Abbot sent one of his monks with him, a young man with a fine muscular body and a face ruined as if by fire. His name was Eisei. He covered his features, what was left of them, with a black silk cloth, above which his lashless eyes darted, like a lizard's. Masachika learned his injuries had been caused in some way by Shikanoko. Eisei was an adept in esoteric practices, which would be useful, for everyone knew by now that Shikanoko was not only a warrior but also a sorcerer.

Their journey was delayed by downpours, flooded rivers, and a kind of sullen hostility among porters, innkeepers, ferrymen, in fact almost everyone they had to deal with. Horses went lame, provisions disappeared, mildew sprang out on everything, reins and tempers snapped. People grumbled openly that the Miboshi lords had offended the gods and they were being punished for it.

"You should cut out their tongues," Eisei said to Masachika.

"Then I would make an entire population dumb," he replied. He pretended to be unaffected by the unrest that seethed just below the surface of everyday life, but as usual he was calculating his best chances. The Miboshi were powerful and well armed, Aritomo single-minded and ruthless, blessed by the support of the Prince Abbot, but if Heaven had turned its face against him . . . Masachika was keeping all possible choices in the balance.

Once again, he passed through the barrier at Shimaura. The Kakizuki skulls had long been removed, but he thought of the living, at Kuromori, now immeasurably strengthened by Shikanoko. They would consider themselves betrayed by him and were no doubt thirsting for revenge.

He learned here that Shikanoko was still at Kuromori, his forces growing in number daily as disaffected and dispossessed men found their way to him. The guards at the barrier were tense and resentful, tired of the constant rain, the flooding river, the gales that kept ships confined to port. They complained to Masachika that their supplies were dwindling, they were too few to fight off an attack, and if they were overwhelmed the road would be cut between Miyako and Minatogura.

Masachika knew he had many failings. He was quite prepared to live with dishonor rather than end his life prematurely, but he did not consider himself a coward. He was aware that most of his small band of men mistrusted him; the disaster of the first raid, in which comrades and cousins had died, was still fresh in their memories, and everyone knew he had spent six months with the Kakizuki. The capture of the Princess, and his rise in standing with Aritomo, counted in his favor, but there were still whispers. *Once a spy, always a spy. A man who turns once will turn twice.* He resolved he would ride to Matsutani openly, showing neither hesitation nor fear. He dismissed the guards' complaints and scoffed at the rumors that Shikanoko had supernatural powers, employed invisible imps and artificial warriors that could not be killed, and talked to the dead.

Eisei took such rumors seriously, explaining to Masachika that that was why the Prince Abbot wanted him alive. "He wants to understand the source of these skills so he can control them himself. Shikanoko has a mask, fashioned from a stag's skull; it gives him all the power of the forest, but only he can use it." He touched the silk veil that covered his face. "It burns anyone else."

"Is that what happened to you?"

Eisei nodded. "Before that, I was my lord's favorite. Now I am disfigured. I bring pollution into his presence. He looks on me with pity. He is good to me, and kind, but it is not pity I want from him, or from anyone. I used to be at his side during secret rituals of great power. He showed me wonders and took me to realms that are hidden from ordinary people. Now all that is barred to me. From time to time he graciously allows me into his presence, but I don't like to accept too often. I am afraid I will infect him with my bad fortune. So I sweep the floors and tend the gardens. It is all I am good for."

"You were lucky you did not lose your eyes," Masachika said.

"If I were blind, I would not be aware of my disfigurement," Eisei replied. "I would not see pity and revulsion on the faces of others. I had lost all interest in life; indeed, I tried to hang myself." He indicated marks at his throat, which Masachika had thought were scars from the same incident that burned his face. "The branch I chose broke. It was not my time. My lord decided to find some purpose for my life and gave me this mission to accompany you."

They rode in silence for a while. The rain had slackened to a drizzle; the mountains were swathed in mist. Biting insects buzzed around them, making the horses shake their heads and kick at their bellies.

"There are some guardian spirits at Matsutani," Masachika said. "Last time I was there they prevented me, or anyone else, from entering. I am hoping to be able to placate them this time."

"Maybe I can be of help," Eisei said. "I know many spells and prayers of exorcism. Who placed them there?"

"An old man, Sesshin. I remember him from my childhood. He lived at Kuromori for many years. We were not aware that he was a powerful sorcerer. After he left, no one knew the spirits were there and so they were neglected and have turned spiteful."

"That can easily happen," Eisei said. "Guardian spirits

can be quite petty and they take a lot of looking after. Sesshin . . . that must be the same old man who now plays the lute in the courtyards of Ryusonji. The monk Gessho captured him and brought him to my lord, along with Shikanoko. He had been blinded and apparently all his powers were gone. He turned out to be a fine musician, though. He and my lord had some past history between them—my lord had been looking for him for a long time. He was not pleased when Sesshin escaped him. He held his physical body, but his sorcerer's spirit had fled with all its powers. And then Shikanoko slipped out of his control, and Gessho was sent after him again, but never returned. It is the first time anyone has challenged the Prince Abbot in this way. That is why Shikanoko must be destroyed."

The rain began to fall more heavily. They spent a sleepless night in a group of hovels that hardly merited the title of village. There was little food other than a thin soup of mountain herbs. Masachika learned that Matsutani was still haunted and that Shikanoko was not there. Lady Tama lived nearby, alone, in theory, though Hisoku's name was mentioned once or twice in a way that made Masachika burn with anger. He had vowed to kill the man at the first opportunity and he hoped it would present itself soon.

The next morning they were met on the road by Hisoku himself, at the head of a band of ten or twelve men. They were all gaunt and ragged. Only two had horses, besides Hisoku, and their weapons were old-fashioned and inadequate. Moreover, they were not ready for battle. Masachika learned afterward that most were Miboshi warriors, probably expecting him and his men to be reinforcements. Had the sun been shining he might have been inclined to negotiate and take the time to find this out, but the rain had put him in a vile temper and the sight of Hisoku enraged him further. He gave the order for an immediate attack.

The men on foot were cut down with swords; the horsemen tried to escape, but fell in a hail of well-aimed arrows. Hisoku's devious skills were no use to him in an open fight. He was swiftly unhorsed, and Masachika ordered his men to hang him from an oak tree on the edge of the forest.

"Make sure the branch does not break," Eisei said.

The branch was secure. Hisoku cursed Masachika, then pleaded, to no avail. They left his body still kicking and struggling and rode on to Matsutani.

14

TAMA

The long, cold winter and the wet spring had given Lady Tama plenty of time to reflect on her situation, and she had realized her life was hopeless. As soon as the rain stopped, she decided, she would return to Muenji, shave her head and become a nun, and spend the rest of her life atoning for the sins she had committed and the hardness of her heart.

Matsutani had been granted to her in a tribunal of law, but she could not take possession of it because it was occupied by hostile spirits. She saw all too clearly the universal law of cause and effect. If she had not taken out Sesshin's eyes and driven him away, the spirits would have remained hidden, protecting the house and the estate as they had done for years without anyone knowing of their existence, save the man who had set them there, the very same Sesshin.

If even the powerful monk Gessho had not been able to control them, she did not think anyone could. Matsutani would have to be abandoned. Already the house was beginning to disintegrate. Most of her treasured possessions lay strewn around the garden, slowly rotting away and probably being possessed themselves by unwelcome elemental spirits. Holes had appeared in the roof, shutters hung lopsided and rattled in the wind, wild animals had made dens under the verandas and birds nested in the eaves. A huge white owl had taken to roosting on the ridge of the roof. It hooted in an unpleasant way throughout the night.

Haru's house, where Tama now lived, was cramped and uncomfortable. Tama felt that Haru despised her secretly, though the woman spoke to her respectfully and deferred to her. The abduction and death of Tsumaru lay between them; just as, while he lived, they had competed for his affection, so, now he was dead, each blamed the other and felt her grief was greater.

They did not speak of Hina. It was another of Tama's regrets, that she had not made more effort with the child, made pale and mute by grief, when Hina had become her stepdaughter. But she had had her own troubles, her brother's death, the loss of her first husband, the new marriage, the pregnancy. Somehow she had overlooked Hina, and when she had finally given her some attention, it was too late. Hina had withdrawn any affection forever.

Tama knew Haru's children disliked her, especially the older one, Chikamaru, whom everyone called Chika. He was an insolent and taciturn boy who came and went without telling anyone what he was up to. She suspected he was going at night to Kuromori, where Shikanoko had been all winter, along with Chika's father, Kongyo, and the rest of Kiyoyori's men. He never told her what was happening there, but sometimes his eyes gleamed when he looked at her and his lips curved in a scornful smile.

And the final reason for giving up and returning to the temple was that she would be rid of Hisoku—she could see no other way to shed him, apart from having someone kill him, and among the few men at Matsutani the only one she could call on to carry out an assassination was Hisoku himself. He believed he was indispensable to her, that his adoration of her gave him some claim over her. He exaggerated his abilities and made much of the fact that he could approach the house with offerings, without having anything thrown at him.

"You don't see that you are their slave," she said. "You are not in any way their master."

"Slowly does it," Hisoku replied. "I am working up to it, just as I am working up to you."

He treated her with increasing familiarity and she knew he expected to be her husband soon. The thought made her skin crawl, yet again she could blame no one but herself. She had played on his devotion, using him to obtain the documents that proved Matsutani was hers, allowing him to accompany her, relying on him to take command of the Miboshi men who had fled after Shikanoko's attack on Kuromori, as if he were her husband and lord. It was only natural he would eventually demand payment. From

Haru's remarks, she knew that everyone thought she and Hisoku were already man and wife in all but name, and this filled her with revulsion, at the same time driving her toward him as if she were under a spell. Her sense of obligation, the lengthening days, the budding of spring, late and cold as it was, her own body with its frank needs and desires, all conspired to weaken her resolve.

In the fourth month the rain lessened, and late one afternoon Tama walked toward the west gate, trying to come to a decision. She resolved she would leave that week, walk to the coast, and take a boat to Minatogura, as she had done a year ago. This time she would truly renounce all earthly desires and cut her hair. A weight lifted from her and she began to whisper her goodbyes to her childhood home, bidding farewell to the living and the dead.

Chika appeared beside her, seeming to materialize out of the drizzle. He was soaking, moisture beading his thick lashes and the smooth skin of his face.

"You startled me," she said, trying to smile.

His stare was unresponsive and cold. "Your man is dead."

"What?"

"Hisoku is dead."

She thought his eyes shone with secret glee. *Let me feel grief,* she prayed, *let me not feel relief.*

"They hanged him," Chika went on.

"Who?" She looked around wildly.

"Some men from Miyako. They are coming here. One of them came before to attack Kuromori. He knew the mountain path because he grew up there. But the defenders were warned." He glanced up at her, unable to keep pride and self-satisfaction from his voice. "He was the only survivor. Can you guess who it is?"

"Masachika," she said. He had been offended and humiliated by Hisoku and now he had taken revenge. To hang him was an outrage. Why could he not have simply taken off his head? She could feel tears threatening. So, she could experience grief—not only for Hisoku but for Masachika and herself, for the married couple they once were and the brief, fierce happiness they had known in the house, once beautiful, now derelict and haunted.

Chika was watching her face. "Is he friend or foe to you?"

"I don't know," she replied.

She composed herself and went to the west gate to wait for Masachika. From the house behind her she could hear the spirits' voices. They sounded agitated.

"Matsutani lady, who are you waiting for?"

"Where is Hisoku? We are hungry and thirsty."

"Is it another great monk, like Gessho?"

"Gessho is dead. He lost his head!"

"Hisoku is dead, too," Tama said quietly.

"Oh yes! Oh yes! Born to be hanged!"

"It's the one that came before, that we sent the bees to sting."

"Didn't the bees kill him?"

"We'll send more this time."

"I beg of you, be still," Tama said, "until we know why he has come."

"You should have been still, Matsutani lady. You should have waited before you tore out our master's eyes."

"Before you turned him out into the Darkwood."

"I regret that with every fiber of my being," Tama whispered.

"Too late, too late, too late!" they both jeered, running the words together.

"Toolatetoolatetoolate."

"I did not expect you," she addressed Masachika when the men rode up and he dismounted. She recognized one of the riderless horses they led as Hisoku's, and the sight of the horse alive, when its master was dead, pierced her unexpectedly. "If anyone came, I thought it would be Shikanoko, who has been at Kuromori all winter."

He bowed his head to her, and gave his horse's reins to the nearest man.

"Shikanoko is indeed the reason I am here."

"Hisoku rode out thinking it was him, making an outflanking attack. You did not need to kill him. You were on the same side!"

"He and his men surprised us in an ambush," Masachika said. "They did not declare their names nor did they have any banners or crests. Anyway, they are all dead now."

"Toolatetoolatetoolate," sighed the spirits.

Masachika glanced toward the garden. "So the house is still possessed?"

"Yes, and they will be more fractious now. Hisoku

she asked, "Masachika, are you with the Miboshi now or are your sympathies still with the Kakizuki?"

"The Kakizuki are doomed," he replied. "Only a fool would side with them. But I am first with Matsutani and its lady."

Tama smiled. "I suppose I have already abandoned the Kakizuki, since it is the Miboshi who endorsed my claim."

"I am Aritomo's man now," Masachika said. "My main task here is to approach Shikanoko on his behalf."

"Shikanoko is nothing," Tama said. "He was a wild boy whom the bandit Akuzenji found in the forest. Your brother spared his life because he considered him harmless."

"He has Lord Aritomo and the whole of Miyako worried about him," Masachika replied.

They passed through the gate and Tama bowed to the eyes and then to each gatepost, murmuring words of thanks.

On the other side the monk Eisei was waiting for them.

"I have come to help you deal with the spirits," he announced.

"The matter is settled," Masachika said. "They are back where they belong."

"But you wanted me to chant and pray." Eisei's face could not be seen beneath the black cloth, but he sounded disappointed.

Behind them they heard whispering. Eisei turned back eagerly. The gateposts were quivering.

"Shikanoko!"

"Shikanoko is coming."

"Who is Shikanoko?" Eisei asked.

"He's—" Masachika began, but Eisei silenced him with a gesture. "I know who he is. But let's hear what they say."

"Shikanoko is our master's heir."

"Yes, our master gave his power to him."

"What does that mean?" Eisei demanded.

"Find out for yourself."

They all heard the sound of horses' hooves and turned toward the east, Masachika drawing his sword.

Tama had described Shikanoko as a wild boy and at first she did not recognize the figure who dismounted from the leading horse. He had not only grown and filled out, he had gained an air of authority. Masachika's men were gathering around them, some with their swords drawn, others setting arrows to their bows.

Masachika said, "Let no one attack. He is not to be harmed."

Shikanoko's gaze swept over him and he gave a slightly mocking smile, but he did not speak to either of them or even acknowledge them. He walked past them to the gate and knelt before the eyes. A strange wolflike creature followed at his heels until one of Shikanoko's companions dismounted and called the wolf to him. His face was horribly scarred, as if by fire.

Tama was aware of Eisei staring fixedly. Eisei took the silk covering from his face and she saw that his scars were identical. Then both young men smiled, their ruined features assuming the same expression, their eyes full of emotion.

Shikanoko stood, his own eyes filled with tears. He

brushed them away and said quietly, "Hidarisama, Migisama, I am glad to see you obedient to your old master again."

Tama knew he was addressing the guardian spirits, though they had given no sign of their presence, and he knew what to call them. Even Hisoku had not known that.

Shikanoko held up his right hand and said more loudly, "Jato!" The sword Masachika was holding flew through the air between them and cleaved to Shikanoko's hand as though it recognized him. He said to Masachika, "How did you come by this sword?"

Masachika shrugged and replied, "It fell into my hands."

Shikanoko considered this for a few moments and then said, "It was your brother's sword, recast for me."

"Kiyoyori's sword? How did you get it? Surely it was destroyed in the flames along with its owner?"

Shika laughed. "Neither the sword nor its owner was completely destroyed." He held it out, and for a moment Tama feared he would cut Masachika down with it there and then. But he said, "I don't think you came just to return Jato to me. You have a message for me?"

She truly admired Masachika at that moment, for, showing no sign of fear, he announced loudly, "I am Matsutani no Masachika, sent by Lord Aritomo, protector of the city of Miyako, to tell you he holds Hidetake's daughter, Akihime, the Autumn Princess. If you surrender and return to the lord you ran away from, the Prince Abbot at Ryusonji, her life will be spared. If you refuse, or if you make any attempt to rescue her, she will be put to death in the cruelest way that can be devised. Also, my lord commands me, if you have any knowledge of the whereabouts of the false emperor, Yoshimori, you are to reveal it to me."

Tama saw Shikanoko flinch slightly at Akihime's name, but all he said was "I don't know where Yoshimori is, but wherever he is, he is the true emperor. Nothing can change that, no matter whom you torture and kill. But you may take my sword in exchange for Kiyoyori's. Its name is Jinan, Second Son, like you, like your false emperor. That is my only message."

15

TAKAAKIRA

While the rain poured down on the capital and while he waited for Masachika to return, Yukikuni no Takaakira reflected deeply on the grievous state of affairs, the imbalance in the realm, the obvious displeasure of Heaven. He tried to put aside his grief for Hina and his anxieties about Masachika to do all he could, for Lord Aritomo's sake, to clarify the problem and put things right.

From time to time he regretted sparing Hina's life. He saw clearly all he had put at stake for her: his position at Aritomo's side, his domain of Yukikuni, his life. He should have had her killed the first time he set eyes on her, in this very house. But then he remembered the delight and joy she had given him, her intelligence, grace, and beauty, and he ached with love and grief. He dreamed that she was alive, and woke with hope, but then knew, if she did still live, he would sooner or later have to arrange her death, and wished for her sake that she had had the swift, gentle death of drowning.

Her presence was everywhere. She seemed to have just departed from each room he walked into. He heard her footsteps on the veranda, her voice in the garden. To escape her, wanting to see again the young woman, Akihime, who was defying both Lord Aritomo and the Prince Abbot, and remembering his intuition that there was some evil dwelling at the heart of Ryusonji, he decided to pay a visit to the temple.

His previous visit had been last summer, just after the first typhoon. Now the heavy rain had settled sullenly over the city. The lake was churned into foam and threatened to brim over its banks and join the river, which was rising every hour to meet it.

The Prince Abbot greeted him cordially, making no reference to the weather, as if by ignoring it he would deny its hostility. He inquired after Lord Aritomo's health and begged Takaakira to convey his messages of respect and devotion.

"We shall soon have reasons to celebrate," he said. "I am sure Shikanoko will attempt to rescue our prisoner. Once we have him under our power, we will soon discover Yoshimori's whereabouts. When they are all dead, harmony will be restored."

But he is the true emperor, Takaakira thought, as he had before, and immediately found himself trying to close his mind to the Prince Abbot's penetrating gaze.

"I would like to see the Princess," he said.

The sight of her, lying in a small cage, her hands bound,

shocked him. He did not understand how she could still be alive. In her twisted limbs and crushed body he saw Hina. This was what Hina would be subjected to if she ever fell into Aritomo's hands.

Let her be dead, he prayed. *Let her be drowned.*

"Was it necessary to be so cruel?" he said to the Prince Abbot, who was surveying Akihime with cold contempt.

"She knows where Yoshimori is and will not tell us. Her stubbornness must be punished, her will broken. And her suffering will reach Shikanoko and bring him to us."

Takaakira gazed on her with pity mixed with revulsion. There were many things he wanted to ask her, not about Yoshimori, but about her time at Nishimi. What had Hina been doing there? Did she still read the Kudzu Vine Treasure Store? How was she progressing with her music and her poetry? Did she talk about him? He wanted to know everything that had happened in the months he had been away. And where was the rosewood box with the old man's eyes? Suddenly he felt he was in danger of breaking down and weeping.

He tried to mask his weakness from the Prince Abbot. The thought of the old man reminded him that he had been going to question him more forcefully, before he had been sent to Nishimi. His excitement at having somewhere to hide Hina, and his absence from the city, had driven it out of his head.

"What happened to the blind lute player?" he said.

"He is still here," the Prince Abbot replied. "He still plays and sings, but his mind is gone."

"I would like to talk to him alone," Takaakira said.

The Prince Abbot glanced at him sharply. "What good can that do? You won't get any sense out of him."

"I want to rule him out as a possible source of imbalance," Takaakira replied. "Perhaps proper restitution has never been made for the wrong that was done to him. We should look at everything."

"You will find him in the cloister, I suppose. You may talk to him on your way out."

There was a dismissive tone to his voice that irritated Takaakira. *This priest is full of arrogance and conceit*, he thought, and found himself wondering if the Minatogura lord might not be better off without him.

Sesshin was under the shelter of the cloisters, sitting cross-legged, his lute on his knees, his face turned upward, his lips moving as if he were praying. The sight of his ancient, eyeless face made Takaakira shiver. This man's eyes knew his innermost secrets, all his mistakes and weaknesses, and had made him weep. Did Sesshin know what his eyes saw, or were they forever separated?

He knelt beside him, speaking clearly in order not to startle him. "Master Sesshin, it is Yukikuni no Takaakira."

Sesshin made no response. Surely he was not deaf, too? He spoke more loudly. "Are you well? Is there anything you need?"

Sesshin said finally, "It is gracious of such a mighty lord to concern himself with my well-being. I have no wants, no needs."

He did not sound at all senile.

He then said, "Are you well, Lord Takaakira?"

"Well enough."

"And Lord Aritomo? Is he well?"

"I believe he is in good health," Takaakira said.

"Tell him to make the most of it, for he will be very sick soon."

"You could lose your tongue or be put to death," Takaakira said warningly, but instead of being intimidated, Sesshin seemed to find this amusing and shook with silent laughter. He nodded his head for quite a while, making Takaakira feel that perhaps his mind was wandering and he was wasting his time.

"Since you were so kind as to inquire after my health," Sesshin said, "I will give you some advice. The Prince Abbot has been very gracious to me lately, but for many years he has wanted to kill me. Do you know why? Because I was the only person ever likely to challenge him. We were equals once, can you believe that? And now he is bringing to Ryusonji the one person who can bring him down. Yes, he is about to fall. Sooner or later Aritomo will follow."

"What are you saying?" Takaakira said. "Is there going to be an attack on Ryusonji? Is it Shikanoko?"

Sesshin took up the lute and played a few plaintive notes. His face, which had been suddenly youthful and full of intelligence, now looked old and vacant again. He began to sing in a mumbling tone. Takaakira could not make out the words, but he thought it was the song he had heard before, about the dragon child. He looked across the courtyard, through the heavy rain, to the lake.

Sesshin sang more clearly:

He sleeps beneath the lake,
The dragon child,
But he will wake
And spread his wings again,
When the deer's child comes.

"Is the deer's child coming?" Takaakira said urgently. "Is it Shikanoko?"

A smile flitted across Sesshin's face.

Takaakira could see he would get no more sense out of him. He bade him farewell, stood, and began to walk to the main gate. The courtyards were deserted and although he could hear chanting from within he did not see anyone. However, just when he had passed through the gate and was making his way to where his carriage was waiting, the ox up to its hocks in mud, he saw coming toward him the young monk with the scarred face who had gone with Masachika.

The monk recognized him. "Lord Takaakira? I am Eisei. You came to visit our abbot last year."

"Yes, I remember you. You have been in Matsutani, haven't you? What news do you bring?"

"Lord Masachika is on his way to Lord Aritomo now."

"Then I must hurry back there," Takaakira said.

Eisei looked around. He seemed nervous, and he fixed his eyes on Takaakira as if he wanted to speak to him but did not dare.

Takaakira gestured to him to move under the shelter of the eaves. The rain dripped steadily around them. The ox lowed mournfully and shifted its legs. "Where is Shikanoko now?" Takaakira said.

"He is not far away. He came at once, as soon as he heard about the Princess."

"Did he send any message?"

"He sent his sword," Eisei said. "It is a sort of message. Its name is Jinan."

"Second Son?"

"Yes, like our current emperor."

Masachika will not dare say that to our lord! Takaakira thought.

"So, how many men came with him?" he asked.

"Just one. His friend, Nagatomo. So many rivers are in flood, it wouldn't have been possible to move a whole army."

"He has made himself vulnerable of his own free will?" Takaakira said in disbelief.

"He will give himself up if the Princess is released," Eisei replied.

"Surely he will attempt to rescue her?"

"Lord," the monk said. "I must tell you. If you or my master have me put to death, so be it. Shikanoko has extraordinary power, far more than my master suspects. If he enters Ryusonji he will destroy it."

It was just what Sesshin had said a few minutes earlier.

"But more important," Eisei went on, "Yoshimori is the true emperor. Nothing can alter that."

"How have you changed your thinking so much?" Takaakira demanded. "You left as a loyal servant to the Prince Abbot—now you will betray him?"

"It is not betraying someone to tell them they are wrong. Maybe it is the highest loyalty. Meeting Shikanoko again opened my eyes. I thought I hated him because my face was burned by his mask, but it wasn't he who deserved my hatred. He didn't force me to wear it. He warned against it, just as he tried to protect Nagatomo." His face changed as he spoke. "We have identical scars," he said. "We call ourselves the Burnt Twins."

"Were you on your way to see the Prince Abbot now?" Takaakira said.

"Yes, I intend to tell him what I just told you."

"Don't do that yet. You will be punished severely. I will talk to Lord Aritomo first. I will intercede with him on Shikanoko's behalf. Can you reach him, perhaps through your friend—Nagatomo?"

Eisei nodded.

"Then tell him to wait until he hears from me. I will come here tomorrow and meet you, at noon. I hope I may be able to save both him and the Princess."

While listening to Eisei's words Takaakira had felt that his earlier misgivings had been confirmed, and he had come to a decision. Ryusonji and the Prince Abbot were indeed at the heart of the country's suffering. It was his duty, and would be his greatest loyalty, to tell his lord. He got into the ox carriage and ordered the groom to go with all haste to the palace.

He met Masachika in the anteroom. It was filled with warriors, seeking to present petitions or awaiting orders. Masachika greeted Takaakira politely enough, spoke briefly of the difficulty of the journey, but there was no time to say more before they were summoned into the inner chamber.

Aritomo looked even more tense and suspicious than usual. A muscle twitched constantly beneath his left eye, betraying sleeplessness. His anger simmered beneath the surface, making both men nervous and deferential.

Masachika took his sword from his sash and held it out in both hands, bowing over it. "Shikanoko surrendered his sword to me and I present it to you, lord."

Aritomo looked slightly less grim as he took it and studied it carefully. "It is very fine. I have never seen anything quite like it."

"I believed it was forged in the mountains," Masachika replied. "Perhaps by tengu, perhaps by a sorcerer."

Are you not going to tell our lord its name? Takaakira thought, but did not speak.

"So, you brought the upstart back with you?"

"He followed us. He is close to the capital now. He came alone save for one companion. I have his assurance he will give himself up if the Princess is released."

"Well done, Masachika," Aritomo said, his good humor apparently restored. "I will give the sword to you as a sign of my gratitude."

Masachika bowed to the ground. "I must also tell Lord Aritomo that I am reconciled with my former wife. I have secured Matsutani and dealt with the hostile spirits that had made it uninhabitable. The estate is firmly in Miboshi hands, and if you trust me I will regain Kuromori and Kumayama, too."

"Lord Aritomo," Takaakira said. "May I speak with you in private?"

Aritomo held up his hand. "Shortly. You dealt with the spirits? How? I know you took one of the Prince Abbot's monks with you. Did he assist you?"

"I did it alone, lord. It was simply a question of replacing something that was lost."

"How mysterious," Aritomo said. His nostrils twitched, his jaw clicked from side to side. "I am no adept. You will have to spell it out for me."

"Kiyoyori's wife, Lady Tama, blinded an old man, Sesshin, a sage. After she turned him out, his eyes were placed over the west gate at Matsutani, where he had previously installed the guardian spirits. After the earthquake, the eyes disappeared and the spirits escaped. I was able to replace them and now the spirits are back where they belong."

"All very satisfactory, no doubt, but how did you come to be in possession of the eyes?"

Takaakira could feel sweat gathering in his armpits yet he felt icy cold. His pulse was beating rapidly.

Masachika said slowly, "Kiyoyori's daughter had taken them with her to Nishimi. I found them there."

Aritomo's eyes bulged. He had been watching Masachika carefully, alert as always to any attempt at concealing the truth. Now he turned his stare on Takaakira.

A wave of heat rose from Takaakira's belly, staining his face red. He wanted to explain what Hina was like, why he had spared her, but, face-to-face with his lord, he knew there were no arguments and no excuses.

"You were concealing Kiyoyori's daughter, all this time?" Aritomo said in disbelief. "Where is she now?"

"She tried to escape while I was securing the Autumn Princess," Masachika said. "It is believed she drowned. But she left behind the box containing Sesshin's eyes."

Aritomo did not seem to be listening. His face was the color of ash; his eyes filled with tears.

"I trusted you when I trusted no one else," he whispered. "We have been close friends for years, all our lives. Is it true that you have betrayed me?"

Takaakira could not answer. His own eyes grew hot. Finally he found his voice.

"It's true that I found Kiyoyori's daughter, let everyone believe she was dead, but spared her and took her to Nishimi. I disobeyed your orders. There was no betrayal, but neither is there any excuse and I am not asking you to overlook, or forgive. Allow me to take my own life; that is my only request. But first I must beg you to listen to me. You are making a terrible mistake . . ." *I am going to die*, he thought, *I can say anything*. But even on the threshold of death he feared Aritomo's anger.

"For the sake of our past friendship I will grant that request," Aritomo said, his voice breaking. "But do it now, at once, or I will burn you along with the Princess."

"Now?" Takaakira said. "Here?" Stray thoughts raced through his mind. *I did not suspect, when I dressed this morning, that I was putting on these clothes for the last time. Now they will be ruined by my blood. I must not hesitate or cringe. I must act bravely. I will never see the Snow Country again. Will I meet Hina on the far side of the river of death? I can do nothing now for Shikanoko or the Princess.*

"You may use the knife belonging to the nobleman Hidetake," Aritomo said with affection, as if he were bestowing a precious gift on his friend.

Takaakira took it, admiring its jeweled hilt, its perfect balance, its folded steel blade of exquisite sharpness. *I will hardly feel it,* he thought, as he unfastened his sash and opened his robes to expose his belly. He felt a rush of tenderness for his unblemished skin, his hard muscles. He felt sorry for his own body and the incurable wound he was about to inflict on it.

"Forgive me," he murmured, and with all his strength plunged the knife in, turned it, and drew it sideways, feeling his own blood hot on his hands. At last he dared to say the words aloud, "Yoshimori is the true emperor!"

He did not seem to feel the cut, but then the agony began. His body, so strong and healthy, refused to die. Aritomo watched till the end.

The last sound Yukikuni no Takaakira heard, as his spirit finally broke free and began its journey across the Three-Streamed River, was Aritomo's sobbing.

16

AKI

One morning Aki heard horses neighing and was convinced they were hers, the ones that had been Shikanoko's, her companions on the road. She could not recognize the girl she had been then, her courage and her freedom. She had been broken by pain, the pain of childbirth, the pain of torture, and by grief for the child she would never see again. But the horses restored a slight flicker of hope. She remembered the night at the crossroads, the ghost that had spoken from the shadows, Kiyoyori, the Kuromori lord. The foal had been born the same day as her son.

The room in which the cage was placed, part of the temple despite the use it was put to, held golden statues of the Enlightened One and wooden carvings of various saints, as well as the lords of Hell. It seemed especially evil to carry out such deeds of cruelty under their gaze. Aki stared back at the figures, wondering why they did not step down from their pedestals and come to her aid.

"Help me," she whispered.

The next day she noticed that someone had placed a catalpa bow among the sacred objects at the statues' feet. She had mourned the loss of her bow, left behind at Nishimi; now as her vision sharpened she realized it was here. It had been miraculously transported to this place. She felt a wave of peace flow over her. It must mean that she had been forgiven. She thought of her ritual box, which she had been given at the same time as the bow, and which she had left with Kai. She comforted herself by picturing Kai and Yoshi as she had last seen them, their life together, the musicians and the acrobats performing around them. If she died now, no one would ever know where Yoshimori was, and she did not expect to live.

She was often feverish. Once she opened her eyes and thought she saw a warrior, one of Lord Aritomo's men, looking at her with pity. But what good was anyone's pity to her now?

For the rest of that day Aki's tormentors left her alone while they turned their attention to another prisoner. From her wooden cage, in the depths of the temple, she could hear sounds that were too easy for her to turn into images. They awakened memory in her own limbs: the crushing rocks, the twisting ropes, the red-hot iron bars. She did not know who this poor victim was. He never cried out or spoke, though after the torturers had finished she could hear the faintest of groans and words of prayer.

She realized she no longer heard the lute music that had been such a comfort to her during her suffering, and she became convinced that the tortured prisoner was the lute player. She grieved for him and prayed for him.

That night she woke soaking and realized she was bleeding. She did not know if it was her monthly bleeding or if the rocks of torture had injured her internally. Her whole body ached dully, the burns interrupting with fierce darting pains. She called for rags and water, but no one came.

She wept freely then, for her child. Bara had tried to tell her something, that Hina had fled with him, but then Masachika had informed her they had both drowned. And she wept for her own life, approaching its end, so brief, so filled with mistakes, grief, and remorse.

A dim lamp burned in front of the statues, barely enough to light the room. For weeks no one had seen the moon. The sky was covered in dense, low clouds and the nights were dark. Shadows flickered across the faces of the statues, giving them expressions of pity and horror.

"It is not pity I need but help," Aki said aloud.

One of the shadows seemed to solidify and stepped toward her. Her heart fluttered, sending pain throbbing through her.

A boy stood at the bars of the cage, his eyes fixed on her.

She half-rose, forgetting the ties, wrenching her arms, increasing the pain so that she could not keep herself from crying out.

He made a sign to her to keep quiet, then moved silently around the cage and knelt so he could whisper to her.

"Are you the Princess?"

She nodded. His nose wrinkled, making her aware of how bad she must smell.

"I am bleeding," she said. "Can you get me some rags and water?"

"Don't worry about that now," the boy replied. "I have smelled far worse than you, believe me."

Even her torturers had not spoken to her so bluntly. They had continued to address her in polite terms and call her Princess, even as they twisted her limbs and burned her flesh.

"Shikanoko sent me," the boy went on.

Her heart thudded and for a few moments she could not speak. "Where is he?"

"Not far away. I am to explore the temple and find the best way to rescue you."

"It is impossible," she said. "Tell him not to attempt it. No one can attack Ryusonji. No one can defy the Prince Abbot."

"You may be right. I had not realized how well protected this place was. It took me a long time to get in, and that was only because whoever set up the protection had not allowed for people like me."

"Who are you?" she said.

"My mother named me Kiku." He moved around the cage, checking the door and the fastenings, loosening the knots that bound her arms. Then he made a slight noise like a gecko and another boy, almost identical in size and looks, slithered out of the shadows.

"Shikanoko told us to bring medicine as well as poison," Kiku explained, squatting down next to Aki. "We didn't do that last time. What have you got, Kuro?"

"What does he need?" the other boy said, peering at Aki.

"*She*. It's a woman, it's the Princess."

"Sorry, it's so dark. I didn't know women got tortured."

"Something to dull pain, and stop bleeding," Kiku said.

"Wound staunch, would that do?" said Kuro.

"Let's try it."

Kuro passed a small flask to Kiku. He turned Aki's head gently and poured the flask's contents into her mouth. It was bitter and viscous.

"Are you poisoning me?" she said.

"We could if you want us to," Kuro replied.

"Don't be an idiot," Kiku said. "Shikanoko wants her alive. That's what *rescue* means. You don't rescue a dead person." Kiku addressed Aki. "There's a lot about being human he doesn't understand. You have to explain everything to him."

"I will be dead soon," Aki said.

"So, we go back and tell Shikanoko not to bother?" Kuro said cheerfully.

"He mustn't risk his life for me," Aki said. "Tell him to find the Emperor. But before you go, can you get that bow for me?"

Kiku went to the base of the statue and picked it up. "Shisoku had some of these," he said. "Are they something magic?"

He thrust it through the bars of the cage. Aki felt its familiar shape, and some courage came from it to her. She twanged the string gently.

At that moment there came a sound from the adjoining room as if someone groaned in a nightmare.

"What's that?" Kiku whispered.

"It is the lute player, I think. An old man who sings ballads and war tales."

"He is being tortured, too?"

"What methods do they use?" Kuro asked. "What causes the most pain?"

Kiku cuffed him. "We'll find out later. Now we have to decide what to do next."

The old man began to sing:

The dragon child flew too high,
He was still so young, but now he's grown,
His wings are strong, his breath is fierce.
His breath is fierce.
He will rise from the lake at Ryusonji.

They all listened without moving. Aki's heart was pierced by the poignancy of the human voice, frail and broken as it was, rising from the suffering and the darkness.

"Nice song," Kiku said.

"I would like to see a dragon," Kuro added.

Then Kiku cried, "Someone is coming!" He grabbed the bow from her.

Torches lit the room, armed monks burst in, running to and fro, searching behind the statues and in every corner, uttering incantations and words of power.

"Who untied you, Princess?" one shouted at Aki.

She made no reply, watching in the torchlight as the boys flitted like bats, appearing and disappearing. Sometimes she could see three or four of them at once, sometimes none at all. The monks herded them, trying to corner them. She saw three trapped, but then one faded as one of the monks grabbed at him, and Kiku jumped up, seized a rafter, and swung himself into the hole in the ceiling through which they must have first entered the room. He called back to his brother and Kuro leaped with astonishing agility to grab his outstretched hand.

Someone spoke a single word, someone standing in the doorway, a quiet, powerful presence.

The Prince Abbot was asserting his authority over his spiritual realm and the intruders who had breached it. But it was too late. The boys had disappeared.

"They escaped, lord," said one of the monks.

"I allowed them to. They will return with Shikanoko."

"What creatures are they? Are they human?"

"Not really. I don't know exactly where they have sprung from, why they have appeared now, but they are at least part demon."

"They could make copies of themselves and disappear into invisibility."

"I have heard of such things," the Prince Abbot said.

"What does it mean?"

"Nothing," he snapped, but Aki thought she heard unease in his voice.

He moved toward her cage.

"She is bleeding," he said. "This place will not be purified until she is burned."

17

SHIKANOKO

Shikanoko, Nagatomo, and the two boys had found rooms on the edge of the city, not far from Ryusonji. Shika traded the horses they had ridden so far and so fast for food and lodging. They were among hundreds of others who were escaping the flooded countryside to offer prayers and make petitions at the capital's many temples and shrines.

That night Eisei sent a message to say he would bring Takaakira to meet Shika the following day, and Kiku and Kuro went to explore Ryusonji. But the boys did not return until after daybreak, and Eisei did not come until late afternoon.

"I waited for Lord Takaakira for hours," Eisei said to Shikanoko. "And then I heard he was dead. Aritomo ordered him to take his own life. The Prince Abbot has had to perform a purification ceremony and the funeral will take place in a few days. Everyone, the whole city, is in shock. He was Aritomo's closest friend and very popular. No one understands the reasons, but it must be because he dared to speak up to Lord Aritomo on your behalf." After a moment, he added, "He was going to help you, I truly believe it. He wanted to spare the Princess and save your life. Yesterday he talked for a while with Sesshin and after that the Prince Abbot put Sesshin under torture, too. I don't understand for what purpose. He is just an old man who is losing his mind."

"I'm surprised he's been so lenient to him till now," Shika said. "They are long-standing rivals."

"But he is helpless now," Eisei said. "Is it because he gave all his power away to you?"

"How do you know that?" Shika asked.

"The spirits in the gateposts at Matsutani told us."

"They talk a lot of nonsense," Shika replied. "And, regardless, I wonder if there is any power in the world that can help me now or save the Princess."

"What will you do?" Nagatomo asked.

"Let me reflect for a while, and then I'll decide."

It had taken Kiku and Kuro a long time to escape from Ryusonji. They had come back overexcited and unusually talkative. Now Kuro was occupied with his poisonous creatures, letting the centipede crawl over his hands and the snake through his hair. Kiku prowled restlessly round the room.

"Do you know, I think I miss Mu?" he said suddenly, coming to a halt in front of Shika.

"I do, too," Shika said. He had been worried about the

other three boys all winter, had sent Chika to check on them once the snow melted, and had intended to bring them to Kumayama to be with him. But now he was glad they were still at Shisoku's place. They would be safer there, when he was dead.

"You must go back to the forest," he told Kiku, "whatever happens to me."

"What is going to happen?" Kiku asked.

"I don't know yet. Leave me in peace for a while. I need to think."

"Well, don't think for too long. He says he is going to burn her."

"That can't take place till after Lord Takaakira's funeral," Eisei said. "So we have a little time."

"What else can you tell me about her?" Shika asked.

"She is very unwell," Kiku said. "I brought her bow. It was on the altar in the room she's imprisoned in."

Shika held it, gazing on it in wonder. He knew it was a source of power to her. "I wish I could take it back to her," he said.

Kiku gave one of his rare smiles. "Maybe we will."

"There is a dragon in the lake," Kuro said.

"Yes, Tsumaru's death awakened it," Shika replied.

"Tsumaru?" Kiku questioned.

"He was Lord Kiyoyori's son. He was just a child when he died."

"Lord Kiyoyori, our father?"

"Yes," Shika said.

"So he was our brother? We should avenge him." Kiku

gave a wide smile, as if both the idea and the word pleased him enormously. "One more thing, speaking of fathers. Sesshin, the old man who plays the lute, he is also to be burned. We must save him, too."

Shika began to prepare himself, using the rituals he had learned from Shisoku and Sesshin. He brought out the mask and purified it with incense, and repeated the ritual for himself and his weapons. He fasted for the rest of the day, and at night sat awake on the small veranda, listening to the steady beat of the rain, calling on his masters and teachers, the living and the dead, Sesshin, Kiyoyori, Shisoku, Lady Tora, to come to his aid.

He heard Nagatomo and Eisei whisper together, quietly, intimately, and the boys have a brief muffled squabble over the snake. Then everyone fell asleep.

Gen lay with his head close to Shika's feet, neither waking nor sleeping, occasionally quivering. At dawn the fake wolf gave a brief, sharp howl. Shika heard birds waken in the great trees that surrounded Ryusonji. Their song signified for him the power of the forest. Everything spoke to him, the birds' call, the wind, the rain, each tree that shook its branches and dripped moisture. Yet he felt all of his own weakness, felt the old ache in his right arm, and then he heard the voice of the mountain sorcerer: *He could teach you many things, but he could not teach you brokenness.* He had not understood what Shisoku had meant, but now he did. Both he and the mask had been broken. He reached out and felt for it with his fingers, tracing the tiny scars where it had knitted together, the broken antler. He placed it on his face and turned his attention to the temple, let it slip under the great shutters, still closed, and through the courtyards and halls he knew so well. *I am coming. Are you there?*

With a jolt he came up against his former master's mind and will and saw for the first time their true immensity, dense and impenetrable, subtle and ever-changing. Nothing he had would prevail against the Prince Abbot, not the mask, not Jato, not the bow, Kodama, the dream echo of Ameyumi. He withdrew, shaken, aware of all he was facing: annihilation or enslavement, agony of body and soul.

He rose and took off the mask, staring out into the garden, longing to flee. Yet he could not. There was no other way but forward, even if it meant he would join Akihime in death. And he had to go in brokenness, not in strength.

A rattle of stones distracted him. Nagatomo had found an abandoned Go board and was trying to show the boys how to play, with rain-washed pebbles they had filched from the garden. The sound recalled his father. He also had staked everything and lost. Now his son was doomed to follow him.

The three of them stared at him with expectant eyes.

"So, what's your plan?" Kiku said.

"I will go to Ryusonji now, alone, empty-handed," Shika said. "You must return to the hut in the Darkwood, as I said. Nagatomo, I release you from my service, if I can even call it that, it has been so short."

"You are joking!" Nagatomo said in alarm.

"That's not a plan," Kiku cried. "Why don't you want us to help you? We got in before, we can do it again."

"He will let you in, but he will not let you out," Shika replied.

"I refuse to be released," Nagatomo said stubbornly. "I'm coming with you."

"I'm trusting you to take care of the boys, and Gen. See that all three get home safely."

"I don't think Gen's going to leave you!" Nagatomo said, and the fake wolf shook its head and said, "Ne-er."

"What about Jato and your mask?" Kiku said. "You're not leaving them?"

"I said, I must go with nothing, as if I am no one. If I die today, Nagatomo may have Jato, and my bow, Kodama, and you and Kuro must take the mask back to the hut and place it on the altar."

"Can we use it?" Kuro said, frowning.

"Only if you want your face burned like Nagatomo and Eisei. Don't try it," Shika warned. "No one can wear it but me."

"Then you should take it with you," Kiku argued. "And don't talk about dying!"

"You know what you said once," Shika replied. "Everyone dies in the end."

"And the Princess's bow, which we went to so much trouble to bring back?" Kuro asked.

That made Shika hesitate, for the bow was not his to dispose of. "I suppose you should take that to the forest, too," he said finally, "if the Princess is also dead."

He knelt before the sword and the mask, thanking them, relinquishing them. He washed his face and hands, untied his hair, combed and retied it, and brushed as much mud from his clothes as he could. Then he embraced the boys and Nagatomo, advised them to leave right away, and went out into the rain-soaked city. Gen padded at his heels, growling under his breath as if he were complaining, but Shika could not tell if it was about the wet or his own actions.

The main gate at Ryusonji was surrounded by worshippers who had come to beg the Prince Abbot to stop the rain. They fell back at Shikanoko's approach, staring at him and Gen in alarm and surprise.

Eisei was just inside the gate, as though he had been waiting for him, and told the guards to let him in.

"You've come alone?" he whispered.

Shikanoko nodded.

"Where are Nagatomo and your boys?"

"I sent them home."

Eisei's eyes widened. "You're just going to give yourself up? I thought you would challenge him!"

"I'm giving myself up in exchange for the Princess's life," Shika replied.

"They will never let either of you go until they find out where Yoshimori is, and will probably kill you then anyway."

"Then we will die together," Shika replied. "Go and tell him I am here."

He waited in the outer courtyard, Gen pressing against his legs.

On the southern side, there was a shrine where a pure

white stallion was kept to be worshipped and honored as a living god. A boy was futilely washing the horse's legs, but the rain splattered them again immediately. The horse stamped impatiently and swung its head around, taking deep breaths. Then it gave a loud whinny, both joyful and challenging.

"Nyorin," Shika whispered, recognizing his old stallion immediately. He wanted to touch him again before he died. He went to Nyorin and held out his hand, not sure how the horse would react to him. Nyorin lowered his head and allowed Shika to embrace him. Then he neighed again, more loudly still. An answering whinny came from the stables. Risu.

She was tied up just inside the entrance. The foal was loose, standing at her side. Risu whickered at him while the foal stared at him with bold, curious eyes.

"Lord Kiyoyori," he said, seeing in amazement the embodiment of the spirit he had called back from the banks of the river of death, all those months ago.

The foal gave a shrill whinny, and Risu nuzzled Shika, as though she had forgiven him.

"Thank you," he whispered.

Eisei returned. "Come with me," he said. Risu whickered after them and the foal dashed from her side to follow them, and then back again, his hoofs scattering gravel.

Chanting came from the main hall, the dragon sutra, its familiar words springing onto Shika's tongue. And then behind them he heard his old teacher's voice, singing plaintively.

"The dragon child, he flew too high—"

The voice was silenced with a blow. Then came the Prince Abbot's voice: "For the last time, you stubborn old fool, tell me how you gave your power to Shikanoko, or I will burn you alongside the princess."

Eisei said, "They are in the interrogation room."

As they approached the room, Shika heard Sesshin say, "It is given. I cannot take it back. And you may burn me, but you cannot destroy me."

"What do you mean?" The Prince Abbot's voice was almost unrecognizable, husky with exhaustion. The interrogation must have been going on all night.

"I found it, my old friend. The secret we had both been looking for, all our lives. The elements that, combined together, cheat death."

"You cannot die?" Disbelief was mixed with envy.

"I don't believe I can," Sesshin said. "Actually, it's more of a burden than I thought it would be, but there is no unalloyed good in this world, just as there is no perfect evil. All is sun and shadow, darkness and light."

"What is this magic?" the Prince Abbot said. "Is it a potion? An incantation?"

"It was written down in one of my books, but they were all burned in Matsutani."

"Do you not remember? Your memory was always faultless."

"I am an old man. I remember very little." Sesshin's voice lightened. "Ah, here comes my boy," he said with delight.

The Prince Abbot spun around to face the doorway as Eisei led Shika and Gen through it.

"Shikanoko," he said, gazing at him. "We have been waiting for you." Shika could not resist the look and felt his will begin to tremble and submit. Then Sesshin's words pierced his mind. *My boy*, he had said. It was the old blind man who was his true master. He felt the nugget of power begin to glow within him.

The Prince Abbot said to Shika, "You have come to surrender yourself?"

"I am already a prisoner to your monk Eisei," Shika said.

"You will submit to me and refrain from challenging me?"

"Show me Akihime, promise to let her go, and I will do everything you ask of me," Shika said.

"You are too late. You should have come earlier. The burning is already arranged. Lord Aritomo will attend it."

"Then you can burn me with her."

He heard a slight sound from the corner and turned toward it. He had not noticed her in the darkness, kneeling, hands tied behind her back, her head thrown back, her slender throat pale. She moved her head and looked at him. In her gaze he saw not trust, or forgiveness, but a steady acceptance of their destiny.

"I will, with pleasure," the Prince Abbot said, the cruelty in his voice now undisguised. "But first I will take from you what I want. Where is the mask?"

"I didn't bring it. In fact, I've sent it away."

The Prince Abbot smiled slightly. "It cannot be sent

away. Remember, I cast spells on it to make sure it would never escape me, and nor will you."

"Nevertheless, I came without it."

The Prince Abbot was silent for a few moments, as if disconcerted. Then he said, "What about those demon boys who were here last night? Have they accompanied you? Are they hiding somewhere?"

"They have been sent away, too," Shika replied steadily.

"I am sure they can be easily tracked down. Eisei reported to me what he learned at Matsutani. Sesshin gave his power to you, though I still don't understand how. Is it through that power that you control the demons, or is it through the mask?"

"Neither," Shika said. "They are my sons. I brought them up."

"Sons disobey their fathers all the time," the Prince Abbot stated, as, from behind, Shika heard his old teacher sigh and say, "That soft heart is going to be your undoing, my boy, just like I said. I told you to kill the demons."

"Bring Sesshin forward," the Prince Abbot commanded. "And the Princess. I want them to watch how I treat those who disobey me, who try to challenge me."

Their hands were untied and they were dragged forward.

"I would have made you my follower," the Prince Abbot said to Shikanoko, "even my successor. Why did you run from me?"

Shika heard the sorrow in his voice. "I will do whatever you command, give you whatever you want, if you will spare Akihime," he said, falling to his knees.

The Prince Abbot made a beckoning gesture. "Come here."

Shika crawled toward him. The priest knelt, took Shika's head in his hands, and, raising it, placed his mouth over Shika's just as Sesshin had done before.

A gong sounded in the distance, and a cloud of perfume and incense enveloped him. For a moment he thought the whole magical process would happen in reverse. The snakes awakened in his veins, the catlike creature yowled in his brain, but they were fighting against being taken from him. Even if he consented to it they would not be released.

He tried to pull away, but the Prince Abbot's grip was too strong. He could not breathe. He felt the teeth begin to bite into him. All the suppressed horror of the secret rituals of Ryusonji welled up.

He heard the Prince Abbot's thoughts as clearly as if he had spoken.

And now I will send you down into Hell!

Through the darkness that was rising around him came the sound of a bow twanging.

He knew at once what it was. Aki's catalpa bow, used to summon spirits. He had left it in his lodgings. How had it miraculously appeared here? In that moment the Prince Abbot released him, throwing him to the ground.

"You still resist me?" he said. "You will not relinquish it to me?"

Sesshin said, as if from far away, "I did give him my power, it's true, and in that very way that you divined when you tried to take it from him. But I haven't taught him how to pass it on, and won't for a long time, if ever."

Shika tasted the blood in his mouth. For a moment he felt so sick and dizzy, he wondered if he could stand. He felt Gen's tongue on his hands, licking, encouraging him.

The bow twanged again. Akihime called, "Dragon Child! Come to our aid!"

Shika turned to look at her and saw not the tortured captive he had seen earlier but a beautiful shrine maiden, powerful, pure, dangerous. A deep relief washed through him. His instincts had been right. Through his brokenness had been manifested her strength.

As he struggled to his feet the air parted and the mask emerged: the branching antlers, one broken, the lacquered surface, the reddened lips, the black-fringed eyeholes. It seemed more expressive than ever. It said to him, *You tried to leave me, but you cannot. Now I am here. Put me on.*

"Put it on," Kiku said, becoming visible right in front of him, holding out the mask in both hands.

The boys had disobeyed him. Kuro had brought Aki's bow and Kiku the mask. The first act might save them, but he feared the second would destroy him. "I don't need it," he said, stepping back, but the mask leaped at him and fastened itself over his features.

Kiku left a shadow of his second self as he slid away.

"Didn't I tell you it would return to me?" said the Prince Abbot, and he spoke a word of power.

Without thinking, Shika countered it with one of his own. He felt something inside him purr with approval and tasted in his mouth a cleansing bittersweetness. But he knew he could not prevail against the Prince Abbot, here in Ryusonji, in the priest's center of power.

Their eyes locked and the struggle began. Shika fought off a new terror as he penetrated deep into the priest's mind and soul. He saw the spiritual forces the Prince Abbot could call upon arrayed against him. He faltered, like a wary stag in the forest, catching the huntsman's scent, conscious of its broken antlers, seeing already the thicket that would entrap it.

Their minds circled each other, searching for weakness. Shika felt the older man's great strength and subtlety. Visions flashed before him, of endless pain and suffering. Demons rose from the underworld to taunt him. "Soon you will be ours," they jeered, revealing to him all the torments of Hell. Ancient sorcerers threatened him. "You have dared to question one of us and rebel against him? Your soul is lost for all eternity," and they showed him the barren, everlasting wastes that awaited him.

Gen, who was as close at his side in this realm as in any other, said, "Something missing."

Shika was holding on to the power of the forest, the world that existed before men were created and would endure long after they had disappeared, a world that reformed and replenished itself endlessly. He called on the stag whose child he had become, on the greatest oak tree and the most delicate clover, the eagle and the hawfinch, the wolf and the weasel, the snake and the centipede. At Gen's words, for a moment, he saw that the Prince Abbot's guardians were counterfeit, a flashy show with no substance, less real than Shisoku's fake animals. Something was missing, something had forsaken the Prince Abbot, now when he most needed it.

The demons and the sorcerers rose in a huge cacophony, screaming at him. Maybe they were fake, but he could not withstand them. Maybe something was missing, but the knowledge was no use to him. He felt the Prince Abbot's rage and, even more disabling, his pity and his regret, the affection of a father, the wise guidance of a teacher, the unmatchable power of the adept—all these were being withdrawn from Shika, the disobedient child, the rebellious disciple. He was on the point of calling out, *Forgive me! I surrender. I should never have tried to oppose you*, when again the gentle twang of a bow cut through the noise and the confusion.

Aki plucked the bowstring again and called, "Dragon Child! Representative of the gods in this place! Forgive me for offending you. Take my life as punishment, but come to our aid now!"

In the distance Shika could hear the foal's frantic neighing. *Tsumaru!* it seemed to cry. *Tsumaru!*

Tsumaru, the dragon child. In that moment he realized what was missing. The Prince Abbot no longer commanded the power of the dragon. Ryusonji itself had forsaken him.

The guardians surrounded him. "Tsumaru is merely a dead child," they wailed. "There is no dragon."

His spirit quailed, his body shuddered. *I am lost,* he thought, *I have failed.*

"Yes," the priest jeered. "In the end there is nothing. This is what awaits you—complete annihilation. You thought you would destroy me, but we will fall into the abyss together."

"At least you will be destroyed," Shika cried with his last shred of defiance.

Then a lick of fire swept through the counterfeits, charring and shriveling them like insects on a burning log. The ground shook. There was a roaring outside and thunder clapped directly overhead. Three lightning balls crashed through the walls and circled the room, crackling and flaring. They all converged at once on the figure of the Prince Abbot.

The fire consumed him instantly in a bright incandescent pillar. The dragon's roar filled the room, sending the monks fleeing in terror. The fire touched Shika's face, but the mask protected him. He fell to his knees, meaning to give thanks, but at that moment a rush of steam from the boiling lake, like a fine scalding mist, enveloped him, clouding his vision. He lifted his hands to his face, but the mask seemed to have fused to his skin. He knew then that the forest had claimed him. It had given him power, and now he must pay for it. That would be the price of destroying the Prince Abbot.

A profound sadness swept over him, as though he already saw all he would lose. When his vision cleared, he looked around the hall. Flames were licking at the roof beams and smoke filled the air. Aki and Sesshin lay on the ground, their faces hidden. Eisei stood against the wall, his eyes reddened.

Sesshin raised his head and called, "Shikanoko! You must kill the demons. I told you before."

"What demons?" Shika said, confused, his ears ringing.

"The imps, the boys. Lady Tora's children."

"They are your children, too," Shika replied. "And mine and Lord Kiyoyori's."

"Act quickly, my boy, or regret it for the rest of your life."

Kuro had gone to Shika's side, as had Kiku. Now Kuro turned, the snake in his hand, and said, "Why would Shikanoko kill us? He brought us up. He is our older brother."

He threw the snake toward Sesshin. It spun through the air, hissing, writhing, its mouth agape, its fangs bared.

It fell short of the old man and seemed to disappear through a crack in the floorboards.

Shika went to Aki, who lay trembling, still holding the catalpa bow, and tried to take her in his arms, but she rebuffed him gently. Again sadness engulfed him. He had lain with her, he had longed for her, but he barely knew her.

"Shikanoko," she whispered. "I am sorry."

"It is I who should apologize to you. Can you ever forgive me?"

"I do forgive you." It seemed she wanted to say more, but her strength was failing. The bow slipped from her grasp.

"Where is Yoshimori?" Shika said urgently. "We will find him and everything will be right again."

"Yes, you must find him. Promise me you will. But I cannot stay now, my life is forfeit."

"No!" he cried, though he could see she was burning with fever. "We can heal you. Sesshin! Kuro!"

No one answered him.

Aki's body shuddered and arched and she cried out. He looked down and saw that the snake had fastened itself to her ankle, its fangs sunk deep, the venom already coursing through her veins.

"Akihime!" he called, seeing her life flee from her before his eyes. He looked around. "Sesshin, master, help her! Kuro, is there some antidote?"

"There is no antidote," Sesshin said. "I warned you."

"You should have kept quiet, old man," Kiku said. "You upset Kuro. When he is upset he likes to hurt people. That's his nature, and mine, too."

Shika was barely able to speak. He could not look at either Kiku or Kuro. "Go," he whispered. "Let me never set eyes on you again."

"But you will see us again," Kiku said. "You know our lives are bound together. You know we carry out your secret desires."

He hardly heard them, nor did he see them, as they faded into invisibility and passed unseen through the doorway. He continued to hold Aki close while his tears pooled behind the mask and spilled like a waterfall through the eyeholes.

"The Princess is dead," Sesshin said.

"No," he wept. "No, she cannot be."

"Lord," Eisei said at his side. "She is gone."

Sesshin said, "Be thankful for this moment, for it is part of your journey. It shows you the true nature of existence. Everything suffers, everything will be lost."

Shika said, "Why should you be spared death, you who

are old, blind, and powerless? Why did you not die in her place?"

"It is not my fate. It is hers and yours. You have come into full possession of your powers. You overcame the Prince Abbot, with her help. The dragon child himself answered her call, then recognized you and helped you. I am proud of you, my boy."

Shika would have killed him at that moment, except that the old man would not die.

Eisei touched his arm. "We must go. The fire is taking hold."

Where shall I go? he thought. *There is nothing left for me.*

Eisei lifted Aki. Her arm moved, making his heart leap with hope, but he saw clearly that life had fled from her.

"What about the old man?" Eisei said. "Will he come with us?"

"No!" Shika said.

"I must stay here," Sesshin said. "My place is at Ryusonji now. I must turn my attention to the Book of the Future."

The outer yard was flowing with water. Nagatomo was waiting with Shika's weapons, Jato and Kodama. Nyorin was stamping and fretting in the shrine. Shika could hear Risu squealing somewhere. The foal cantered up to him, its eyes huge and dark with meaning.

He took the sword and the bow from Nagatomo and said, "Untie the white stallion and the brown mare."

"But they belong to the horse god," Eisei said.

"They were my horses before that. They will be mine again."

He hoped the horses would attack and kill him, but Nyorin came with him docilely, and Risu followed, calling out to him in her old way.

They fastened Aki's body to the stallion's back. All three horses lowered their heads and moisture formed in their eyes as though they were weeping.

The water came up to their hocks as Shikanoko led them through the flooded city. The deer's child was returning to the Darkwood.

AUTHOR'S NOTE

The Tale of Shikanoko was partly inspired by the great medieval warrior tales of Japan: *The Tale of the Heike*, *The Taiheiki*, the tales of Hōgen and Heiji, the *Jōkyūki*, and *The Tale of the Soga Brothers*. I have borrowed descriptions of weapons and clothes from these and am indebted to their English translators Royall Tyler, Helen Craig McCullough, and Thomas J. Cogan.

I would like to thank in particular Randy Schadel, who read early versions of the novels and made many invaluable suggestions.

All four volumes of Lian Hearn's
The Tale of Shikanoko will be published in 2016.

EMPEROR OF THE EIGHT ISLANDS
April 2016

AUTUMN PRINCESS, DRAGON CHILD
June 2016

LORD OF THE DARKWOOD
August 2016

THE TENGU'S GAME OF GO
September 2016

FSG Originals
www.fsgoriginals.com